Chaos
In The
Mine
Township

DAVID KATULWENDE
INSPIRED BY TRUE EVENTS

authorHOUSE®

AuthorHouse™ UK
1663 Liberty Drive
Bloomington, IN 47403 USA
www.authorhouse.co.uk
Phone: UK TFN: 0800 0148641 (Toll Free inside the UK)
        UK Local: 02036 956322 (+44 20 3695 6322 from outside the UK)

Published by AuthorHouse 08/12/2020

ISBN: 978-1-5462-9953-0 (sc)
ISBN: 978-1-5462-9952-3 (e)

Print information available on the last page.

This book is printed on acid-free paper.

To my daughters Danielle and Eleanor

Contents

Chapter 1

J was looking forward to entertaining this beautiful girl I had met three days before. We had just been watching my local team beat the visiting team at the Mogadishu Stadium. Any football crazy person knows how thrilling a win in football is. I was delighed as Mwila seemed to enjoy watching football as I did. When the game was over, we exited the stadium opposite the L Section and walked through the compound streets teaming with miners as it was half-past four in the afternoon almost time to exchange shifts. We saw vendors pushing wheelbarrows to and from Chamboli Market. A few children flew kites in an open area.

As soon as we passed the Housing Office, three boys came running. "Lumba, would you know what the boys are running away from?" Mwila asked me, pointing at them. I did not know the answer and growled in a deep, muffled voice. "No."

The boys yelled something Mwila and I could not understand. They attempted to open the gates they came across, but all the gates seemed locked. It was unusual for the residents to close their gates during the daytime. They were hospitable all the time. It was typical for a visitor to knock, open a gate, go inside the yard and ask for water to drink.

"It is the safest place to live in," the township people would say. To the contrary, on this day, the boys had no luck at all.

"Help!" they shouted, but no one answered. No gate opened.

"Is there a street fight going on, Lumba," a bewildered Mwila asked me.

"I do not know." I held her hand to stop her from walking on ahead. We stood still wondering what was unfolding in front of us. When I looked at a window of the house opposite us, I noticed a curtain move. The image peeping was of a surprised woman. She seemed uncertain when she saw us in the street — her radio tuned to the same channel as her neighbours. It was like every house had a speaker plugged to the amplifier at the Mogadishu Stadium. Initially, I thought the announcement was on football, but it could have been about anything. I knew commotions tended to arise at the end of the football matches. However, when we left the stadium, I did not notice any problems. So, I wondered what the announcement on the radio was all about.

"Lumba, can't these people hear what's going on outside," Mwila's voice squeaked. She leaned against me, and I held her protectively.

Fear showed on the faces of people as they passed. They did not say anything to us, but our eyes were on them. They dashed past us like impalas being chased by a pride of lions.

At a corner of the street, they turned and vanished from our view.

The street was empty once more. It was quiet and still. Wire cars and clay dolls lay on the road. Empty *Saladi* cooking oil containers for the game of *chidunu* scattered around. I guessed, "When the five o'clock mineshaft alarm wails in the afternoon, the children would be back from school and turn the road into a playground once again."

And before we reached the end of the road, I heard a strange noise ahead of us. The shouts grew louder and closer. A crowd emerged, running, shouting, and pointing. They ran the length of the residential street searching for open gates, but they could not find any. Some turned into side roads and disappeared from our view. Unsure of what was going on, Mwila and I flattened ourselves against the *lunsonga* hedge. I could feel myself sweating. We knelt slowly, hand in hand, careful not to break the stalks of the toxic green plant.

"I am afraid, Lumba," Mwila whispered, holding on to me tightly.

"I don't think it's a street fight. Something worse is happening," I called out over my shoulder. My eyes fell on Mwila's arm that was shaking like a leaf. I could hear my heartbeat as we knelt still behind the hedge.

I stared around the street, which I knew very well. I used the road many times on the way to the parish or the stadium. I knew the colours of the houses, the homes that had wooden gates or not, the colours of the curtains on the windows and the roofs with television aerials. Nonetheless, that knowledge was of no use at that moment, and all I could hear were screams.

3

"*Isuleni geti* (Open the gate!). *Twafwa kuno* (Help)". Their running feet were getting closer and closer to us, and they were kicking the closed gates. Mwila's breathing was shallow and fast. I could not imagine what state she was in, and I had no idea what to do. All I wanted was to get her safely through the L Section. So, I stayed still, worried.

The shouts soon faded off in the distance, and the street became quiet, but the fear remained within me. My knees were shaking.

Gradually, we began to feel safe and pulled ourselves from the fence.

"Mwila, it is quiet now. We can go," I was showing some courage that I did not feel.

When we rose to go, I noticed the music from the Nkote Club had ceased. The drums had stopped beating, and the guitars were not strumming. The Masasu band had fallen silent, and radios in the neighbourhood were not playing too. It was quiet.

Then a high-pitched voice called out from across the fence. It was the voice of a woman. "Hello!" the woman called again. Mwila and I looked at each other.

"Hello, neighbours. Heard the noise? It is too quiet now. What is going on out there?" the woman asked.

Suddenly a door opened. The woman came out in a chitenge with praying hands printed on it. She must have been catholic for that was worn by the women's fellowship in the Catholic Church. I was going to talk to her when Mwila pulled me back suddenly. I acquiesced.

Gradually, I felt a welcome feeling of calm had set in as we strolled on the gravel road. Now no one was running, the street was quiet. Gates opened one by one. Swinging inside the yards, the gates clicked to let out the families. They looked at us strangely. Walking cautiously and looking over our shoulders, we mingled with the puzzled faces. The residents seemed to know each other, for they talked among themselves in whispers. I hardly understood what they were saying. They appeared confused just as much as I was. So Mwila and I hurried towards the P Section where we lived.

On our way, as we edged out of the L Section, we came to a full realisation of the panic. The shop corridors on the other side of the Kalukungu Road were a hive of activities. Tailors, watch repairers and shoe cobblers gathered their belongings from the shop verandas, shoving them inside the shops.

"Do not cross the road! Do not cross the road!" shouted a man. His breath was rapid, and sweat dripped from his face.

"Come over this way. Follow me. I live near here. My house is two streets away," he said.

We followed him being led more by his gestures than his failing voice. Pointing and circling his hand in the air. When Mwila looked at me, I shrugged my shoulders. We asked no questions but kept following him. At first, we walked fast, then we got into a jog, but as tensions were building up, we started to run. And he took us back into the L Section.

Then an incredible thing happened. There was a bang; the sky lit up red. White fumes followed "Things do not look good. A mine strike probably," I heard someone across the fence say. I quivered at this suggestion. When I looked up, the sky was white. The *matambula*, mango, avocado, guava, and banana trees in the yards were almost invisible. A thick layer of dense white smoke engulfed them.

We stopped running. I turned my gaze to our saviour, and to my horror, I saw panic on his face. It seemed to me he was lost.

"I live in the next street. We need to find a safe way. You can stay at my house for the time being."

Dogs barked simultaneously from several houses. I worried that a dog might escape and come after us. I knew some fences were porous, and we would not have anywhere to hide if a dog chased us. All the time, the dreaded fumes were descending over the houses.

"This way! They are coming from that direction." I could not get used to the shouts. They multiplied as more people poured into the street. A crowd running from the direction of the P section surrounded us.

"Do not go that way!" shouted another, pointing in the direction of Nkote Club.

Breaking away from the crowd, we followed our guide into a narrow, dusty road that lay between tall hedges of *lunsonga*. I noticed another path. The smoke hung over the L Section like a shadow. All the houses looked exactly alike as the white smoke wrapped them round. "We are lost!" I said more to myself than Mwila and our guide.

Losing my bearing, I began to feel claustrophobic. I was now following the man blindly hand in hand with Mwila. The man led us through a meandering path, and we emerged back into the Kalukungu Road.

"We have come full circle. This man does not know where to go. We are trapped," said Mwila in panic. We considered our options; to abandon his lead or stick with him. "How could we go out of here? Do we know the way?" I considered our course of actions in vain.

I looked up across the road. Desperate people were running. Women with babies on their backs were struggling to balance possessions on their heads. Children cried, holding on to their mothers' chitenges. Market vendors dragged sacks of their merchandise from the market. They scattered in all directions, calling out for help. Some of the baskets and bags opened and items sprawled on the highway. The running mothers and market vendors were too scared to get back to pick them up.

At one point, a flying object landed near us. There was not a sound alongside the fiery red device.

"Lumba, my eyes sting," Mwila cried to me.

"My eyes sting too."

The object exploded, and smoke went wreathing through the air. It was a tear gas canister.

Tears rolled freely from my eyes. We ran about in search of water, shaking gates that did not open. The residents of the L Section had gone back into their houses and closed the gates. We were stranded. The man that had offered to lead us to safety was no were in sight. I saw hopelessness on people knocking at closed gates.

Just then, I saw a man a few houses away. He might have sensed that Mwila and I had nowhere to go. He shouted from a distance, "The gate at the next house is open. It is my house. Go inside quickly."

A group of men and women went ahead of us. We followed them through the gate into the yard and through the door into the house. The host rammed the door shut and drew the curtains.

Chapter 2

"*B*wana, they must be hiding *pafupi chabe*." That was a junior reporting to his boss that whoever they were looking for was somewhere nearby. The Nyanja words confirmed the police presence.

The realisation did not give me any peace, as I felt that we were stuck. With fear engulfing me, I searched the faces in the room. Some were familiar people I saw every day going to the shops, mineshaft, stadium, clinic, library or the famous Chamboli Market. The names of their children came to my mind. I recalled if they kept a dog or if they owned a television set or not. I guessed some of them had seen me before as well, although I could not tell if they knew Mwila. Some were strangers to me, though the township was not very big.

As I contemplated what was unfolding, Mwila looked like an old childhood friend. "That's how trust develops," I guessed, "When you go through problems together, you are no longer strangers to each other. Somehow you begin to look at each other as friends bonded together by misery and pain." Yet, four hours ago, at the Mogadishu Stadium, we were awkward with each other.

"My parents had moved from the M Section a few months ago."

"My favourite team is the Little Chiefs Football Club."

That's all she had said then, her arms were resting on her laps, and she had kept a safe distance from me.

There was no way she could do that now. It was jam-packed, leaving no room for modesty. Her arm was resting on mine. I wondered how long it would have taken us to hold hands had we made it to Nkote Club without the kerfuffle. At the back of my mind was the worry for her safety. Nothing bad should happen to her; otherwise, I would be in serious trouble. I held Mwila close. I had never sensed responsibility as I felt for her at that moment. I just had to get her home to her parents safely somehow.

On the wall above the sofa, a picture revealed a family of six—three boys and three girls. I presumed they all resided at the same abode. None of them was in the sitting room, as I did not see anyone that resembled the faces on the photo except the man that let us in. Maybe the police blocked them on the way from the market, shop or school. There was no way to know.

Around the corner of the house, I noticed a small kitchen. Hunger can sharpen one's senses. I could smell well-cooked beans and *nshima*. This sweet sensation was rudely disturbed by a pungent smell of tear gas that shot through the sitting room.

A few minutes later, a continuous firing of tear gas canisters erupted, and the sitting room shook. A steady stream of the gas was filtering in the house. Then, what seemed a live gunshot followed, and our hiding place went deathly silent. At once, Mwila clutched at me, calling my name in fear, "Lumba!" I jolted.

We started speaking in whispers and gestures, and tears were streaming from our eyes. Moments passed. I heard no voices. But heavy breathing, sneezes, and coughs echoed between the walls. With the gestures completely taking over from the whispers, the gazes revealed searching minds.

And then, noises from the street began to enter the room. We looked at each other for answers, but no one was talking. Heavy feet hurried near our safe house. I could not be sure of the direction they were coming from. "Help!" We all heard the call, looked at each other, but no one moved. I guessed we all felt safe and secure inside, and no one was willing to rock the boat.

"What's going on?" the host finally asked to no one in particular. We looked at each other for answers, but it was clear that no one had a clue about what was happening and why.

One woman had a child on her lap, covered with a dusty-looking chitenge. She kept opening the covering as the child coughed violently. When the child whimpered, the woman cleared her throat, and we turned in her direction. She swung her child, bringing the infant to her breast. The child clasped the nipple between its toothless gums as the mother started explaining. "A lorry belonging to Chimanga Changa Milling Company has been looted. A wheelbarrow hit the lorry and stalled it. I do not know if it was an accident or something worse."

She seemed to have the answers to what had been puzzling us all along. "Boys, girls, men, and women, everybody descended on the lorry. Market vendors left their market stalls and joined in the looting; their customers followed suit. Security guards jumped on the truck. Miners joined too. They emptied a three-trailer load of mealie meal bags." She paused and looked around the room. It was quiet.

Then a man in the corner of the house asked. "Is it a miners' strike?" I felt he echoed my fears. Not that I was sure, but it was the murmuring I had heard earlier across the fences and on the street. And it was a sensible question to ask in a mine compound. Miners striking was more than staying away from work. It spelt chaos in the mine compound. Riots and looting among them. As a realisation dawned on me, I sat up in the sofa gazing the faces.

"It does not sound like it," answered another. I nodded. I had seen armed troops before sent to quell a riot in the compound, but this did not seem like one.

"It feels like a riot to me," someone said.

"Miners' strikes have become frequent now."

"Chamboli is not the same anymore."

"A lot of people have been complaining."

"The mining company are not maintaining roads, houses, streetlights and so on." Listening to the exchanges, I thought it was always the same thing. Time and time again, miners wanted better living conditions.

"The wages are low."

Voices wove in from everywhere.

"What happened to the driver of the milling truck?" Someone enquired.

Until then, I realised my estimation of fifteen adults in the room was understated. More stranded souls were hiding behind the sofas and corners of the sitting room designed to host not more than ten people.

"The driver ran away as the looters got on the lorry. A woman said. She looked like she wanted to say more, but her child was distressing, and her voice was failing.

"About the mealie-meal off-loaders? Did they stay?"

"I do not know," cried the woman rubbing tears. I could not tell if she was traumatised from seeing the looting or toxic gases or the crying child.

I turned. Mwila's mouth was open. She seemed in need of air. I held her shaking hand, and I felt guilty for not being able to protect her.

A man next to me sniffed. I turned and recognised him from the street a while ago. He had failed to guide Mwila and me to safety. He looked familiar now that we were on the couch together. The feeling of urgent need to remember him was waning fast, and I just let an impression of him etch on my mind. I thought he knew something we did not. But he was silent.

"He knows the streets not to pass and the sections not to go to," I wondered as I appraised him from the corner of my eye.

"The paramilitary police are firing tear gas canisters from Chamboli Market," the woman resumed talking when the noise outside subsided.

"They are chasing the looters, following trails of the spilt mealie-meal," she added.

"The military police have been deployed in all the sections of our township and are travelling in IFA trucks." She counted her fingers as if not to miss any section in the compound.

"*Bali ku* H, J, K, L, M, P, *ku ma* New, *na ku* Teachers' compounds." How she would know all the details did not

12

bother me. There was no one with the information except her. So we listened in silence hanging on every word she spoke. Then, the woman stopped talking and looked in my direction.

"Where did you get those boxes from?" She pointed at the cartons, and immediately the silent man shifted his weight on the sofa. He sniffed and pulled the boxes closer to himself.

"Erm—," he stammered.

"What's your name?" asked the woman.

"Hector," he said.

"Where did you get the boxes from, Hector?"

Hector began to explain, but the woman cut him short.

"I know!" she said. Everybody in the room was attentive as she continued, "The shops have been looted. The men and women that ransacked the truck broke down the doors to Fyonse General Dealers shop." She paused. Her eyes fell on the corrugated cardboard boxes. And then she stared at Hector.

I looked at the boxes that stood an arm's length from me. If I had seen the packages before, they had meant nothing to me. Fear came upon me. Then, I felt Mwila pushing closer to me. She put her head on my shoulder like a trusting child. As I looked around the room, all eyes were on Hector.

The woman coddled her baby tightly as if Hector would run riot in the house. The windows began to shake. Eyes moved from Hector to the window. Lifting himself carefully from the seat, the host stood thoughtfully for a while, and then strolled towards a window.

As soon as he peeped outside, a canister hit the wall

near the window. We heard shouts of, "Fire! Shoot!" The paramilitary police obeyed their commanders, and I heard canisters exploding. Smoke filled the air. We screamed and coughed. We cried with tears, and then we cried with anger.

"Where is the tap of water?" cried someone.

"Kitchen!" yelled the host.

"My baby! My baby!"

We pushed each other towards the kitchen. A door opened. The child wailed, and the woman disappeared through the door. I held Mwila tightly and tried to follow suit. Almost everybody seemed to have the same idea, but we found ourselves outside in full view of the paramilitary.

"Fire!" The canisters rained on us in the yard from an IFA truck. We returned into the house, and the host closed the door with a sharp bang. There were bursts of wailing and screaming. A container of cold water went around the room, and table cloths became towels. I looked around, Mwila was still with me, but the woman with the baby was gone. I hoped she had escaped to safety.

"They are after him!" someone pointed at Hector. A few more voices joined.

"Yes. It is you."

"It is him."

"It's because of you!"

A chorus of voices yelled.

"Shh," hissed the host, leaning forward. He pointed towards the neighbours.

We became quiet and listened to the screams from the next-door calling for help.

"If the police *knew* Hector was here, why were they shelling the next-door house?" I thought quietly.

No one said anything as we listened to the screams and calls of help from the surrounding houses and streets. *"Mayo wandi mutule!* (Help!)" They screamed in terrified voices.

In the middle of the bombardment, sirens set off somewhere further away. I looked around the room. Tear stained faces stared back at me. No one was accusing Hector now. I heard a curse, and I listened to a prayer. Mwila and I huddled in a corner, sharing a table cloth.

After what appeared like a long time, the situation seemed to be improving. Some sort of sanity seemed to be returning outside. I heard IFA trucks moving. Canisters exploded further and further away, and the police shouts faded off in the distance until we could not hear the explosions anymore.

The host opened a window, and we began to move about as clear air swept in the house. Feet shuffling became frequent, and sniffles became less. We stared at each other helplessly. It took a long while for all of us to sit up.

"Everything okay?" I said in a muffled voice.

"Lumba, my father," Mwila started to cry, facing me. I felt bad.

I waited a few seconds and enquired, "Is your father alright?"

"I promised to visit him at the J Clinic," she sobbed, wiping her eyes with her fingertips.

"It's alright," I consoled her as best as I could.

"Can we go out now?" she said.

I offered her my hand. Mwila took it and steadied herself to move.

"Thank you," she said, looking at the host.

"The compound is not safe. Please stay a little longer," protested the host.

"I need to see my father," she said.

"If you must," replied the host.

"Careful!" shouted Hector, placing the cartons on the space I had vacated from.

Chapter 3

Chamboli Mine Township had several taverns, clubs, churches, schools, markets and a stadium. The area had a clinic and maternity venue too. With a population of two thousand people, it was the second biggest mine township on the south side of the mineshaft. So, when Mwila told me her father was admitted at the J Clinic, I knew where we were headed. It was a reasonable distance from the L Section. But, under the circumstances, I was not sure we would make it safely.

By the time Mwila and I got out of the yard, the sun had gone down. The beautiful orange glow of the sunset lingered on the horizon, giving Chamboli a mysterious colour. The west of the compound had some light, and the rest was in semi-darkness, exposing different dark shapes. Even the disappearing clouds added to the novelty.

The streetlights started coming on. It was a signal that it was past six o'clock in the evening. The clean night air rushed into the township from the forest. It felt nice to be able to breathe freely at last. We trekked down an empty street to the sound of crickets that had gathered around lamp posts.

Township people started emerging from their hideouts. Some kept their noses covered with wet mutton cloth — the type offered for free by the mining company to their underground miners.

"They are using *spanki* (mutton cloth) as face masks?" I said, but Mwila did not answer me.

Some people did not dare to venture outside their gates. They watched the streets from the safety of their gardens.

"Come inside here!" they invited us.

"No, thanks," Mwila said. She looked distressed and preoccupied.

"Did Hector loot the shop?" I asked. There was silence.

"Did he do it?" I said again.

"Who are you talking about?" she said absentmindedly.

"Hector! I mean, Hector!" I said in earnest, trying to keep her into a conversation.

"What about Hector?"

"Did he break a shop?" I asked. Mwila shrugged her shoulders, saying nothing.

We walked briskly. The houses were now behind us. Emerging on the tarmac, we followed the Kalukungu highway. It was deserted.

"Oh, gosh!" sighed Mwila. "Lumba? Boxes and carrier bags? Look!"

"It is the loot from the shops!" I said.

"They dragged everywhere," I added. My heart began to race.

I had not expected that I would see such wreckage. It was all chaos. What was I supposed to think? Then there was Mwila's safety to consider. I became nervous.

Crossing the road, we walked quickly. The mutuntulwa

trees stood in rows on either side of the road, overgrown branches extending to the streets. Mukuba Mining Corporation had not maintained them either. The white lime painted on the tree stems had turned grey.

And now I could hear the noise. "Mwila, can you hear the underground ventilation fans from the M Section?" I asked, trying hard to keep her in a conversation. I thought that would reduce her tension. I worried she was upset about not being with her father.

"I did not know the fans can be heard from here."

"The ventilation fans are blowing air from the underground mine."

"How did you manage to live in the M Section with such noise?"

"What did you say, Lumba?" came the response. I could tell she was not in the conversation.

I tried to bring her in again, "Are the fans blowing dust and toxic gases?"

"Yes," she said.

"Are they worse than the tear gases?" I asked. Mwila turned and glared at me. Her face was so tense that I got worried I had said something to upset her. And I decided to say nothing for some time.

Once we passed a block of shops opposite the Kalukungu highway, the extent of the damage began to show. Dirt and debris littered the corridors, and broken glass lay on the floor. Doors were closed, and some were open.

The sound of a vehicle jolted us to the present. "Did you hear the engine, Lumba?" she asked.

"Yes, it sounds like an IFA," I said, and we began to run. I saw the lights of the truck and instinctively grabbed Mwila's hand. We flattened ourselves behind the mutuntulwa trees. The noise faded away quickly. After that, we decided not to take the highway and turned into an alley in the K Section towards the J Clinic. A yell of delight went up from the children. They called to each other, picking up the looted items scattered on the road. We stopped to watch, and I wondered aloud if we could pick some items. "Can we search for something interesting?"

"Let's not do that Lumba. Someone might think we are looters," said Mwila coolly.

"Good idea, Mwila," I said.

"Maybe that's what happened to Hector," I said.

"Yeah," she said.

We turned into a footpath that was dark and too small for an IFA truck. For a moment, I felt a bit safe. As we progressed in silence, my heart began to skip beats in fear. I could sense Mwila was afraid too. I dreaded the thought of a paramilitary officer appearing in that narrow passage. We would have no escape, and worse of all, there would be no one to help us. I began to look around the fences on both sides for an escape route.

"Are you okay?" I asked Mwila. I was tempted to hold her hand but decided against it in case she thought I was trying to take advantage.

"Yes. Yes, I am okay but worried."

"We will arrive safely," I said.

"I don't know if we will make it in time," Mwila responded.

"Don't worry about that. We will at least have five minutes with your father before visitors time is over."

Then, I stopped walking.

"Can you hear something, Mwila?" I enquired.

She stopped too for a minute.

"Where Lumba?" She started walking again.

"Wait!" I cautioned.

Mwila turned to look at me, and I saw nervousness on her face.

There were footsteps, but I could not tell from which direction. We looked over our shoulders. The path was dark and quiet, and I felt that it was closing in on us. *Ulunsonga* seemed to be reducing the way, and the trail seemed to come to a dead end.

I had a moment of panic, worrying this girl depended on me for protection I groped for Mwila's hand and found it.

Dull thuds got close. I had never been in a serious fight before. I prayed whoever was following us would not require me to fight. It could be someone harmless. That gave me a lifeline. Gradually the noise was fading. I breathed a sigh of relief.

Dark clouds gathered around and hung low accompanied by chilling cold winds. I could see no stars and the moon hid behind the dark clouds. As we walked, the wind increased steadily, tossing the leaves of the mutuntulwa trees. We walked briskly, breathing in the fresh night air from the forest. The clouds got darker and more massive, threatening to let down their heavy load any time. I could hear thunder in the distance.

Flashes of lightning revealed the mineshaft across the Kamatemate Stream. The two big wheels were spinning. They were much bigger than the wheels of the IFA lorry that had invaded the compound. Then, a loud, dull mine alarm sounded.

"It is nine PM now, Mwila," I said. Everyone in the compound knew the time the mine alarms sounded. Several things were certain in the township. The mine alarms were just one of them. Unless trouble happened underground or in the open pit, what we heard, at nine o'clock was the last alarm we would listen to for the night. That was the routine that was as sure as day and night.

With the alarm came heavy rains. It was like the loud alarm had also commanded the clouds to let go of the load they were carrying. The rain fell quickly, relentlessly soaking our faces and battering the leaves. Then Mwila flung open her umbrella, and I held it up for her. We both huddled together under it.

The rain became heavy as the wind drove the clouds over the mine compound spreading the showers. It was like God had sent the rain to clean the air and remove the tear gas. Though that was a pleasant thought, the rain had managed to slow us down considerably.

The next flash of lightning was longer and brighter. It revealed the J Clinic ahead and an IFA police lorry on the road. We stopped.

"Is there any other way to the clinic?" I asked.

"Not one I am aware of," said Mwila.

"What shall we do?" I asked helplessly.

We considered our options staring into the darkness of a thick cloud cover. Thunderclaps increased. The speed of the wind was growing too, pulling the umbrella from my hand. Mwila helped me hold it fast against the wind. The clouds were still offloading the rains. Pools of water formed quickly filling up the drainage and overflowing on to the road. The ground was slippery, and the way was dark.

Occasional lightning would strike, revealing how distant the J Clinic was from us. We were not close to solving our problem on how we would make it to see Mwila's father.

My shoes were soaked, and the hem of my trousers dripped water. The wind raced, and the trees were dancing to the tune of the blow. We strode beneath the line of mutuntulwa tree. Some small branches broke off, and the current dragged them on to the road. The furrows were overflowing. Rainwater flowed towards the Kamatemate River. By then we could barely see the road marks.

Short of any plans, we trudged up the road through the rainwater with my heart beating against my tight chest. I lowered my head, adjusting a lever on the handle of the umbrella to cover us both better.

My voice was only just audible above the hammering of the rain. I turned around to see my new friend looking worried.

"What has your father been admitted into the clinic for?"

Mwila did not answer. Instead, she looked towards the clinic. Her shoulders dropped, and her whole body looked defeated.

"We cannot make it today," she said in a tone of hopeless surrender. "The gate to the clinic is closed."

"The visiting time is over," she added.

"We can't give up now," I said, trying to give her hope.

"I can talk to the *kanyangus* on duty. I am sure the mine police would understand why we are late."

"Can't you see it's of no use. We have the police right in front of the clinic and the mine police or *kanyangus* as you call them. To make matters worse, it is past visiting hour. Who will listen to your pleas? In any case, I am dripping wet. I would not want my sick father to see me looking like this."

"I agree," I said, looking at my trousers. "I am soaked too."

Mwila pointed in the opposite direction of the clinic. Holding her hand, and the umbrella, we darted around the fields and the footpaths towards the K Section passing the Mogadishu Stadium. The children were no longer in the street. The clutter was floating in the furrows.

We made it back to Kalukungu Road. As we took the corner, an IFA truck flashed the lights ahead of us. Mwila grabbed the umbrella from my hand, closed it and sprinted across the road towards the shops. I followed close behind her.

The verandas at the Asian Shopping Store were lit, attracting insects and flies. We sat and leaned against the glass windows, dripping rainwater. The low hum of the rain intensified the quiet of the night.

We hid behind a pillar when a green military vehicle roared on the mine road. It was breaking branches and leaves on its way. We sat in silence, watching the trees fighting the rain and the wind. I thought it would take a while longer for the rain to ease off. Gradually, the wind carried the clouds, the showers, and dust away from the township.

At last, the wind eased, the rain stopped, and the sky was cloudless. I could see stars twinkling in the dark sky. As the light flickered from the ceiling of the Asian Shopping Store, insects began their orchestra of night sounds. I heard a night owl hoot. It was bewitching and ghastly. Immediately, we hoisted ourselves from the shop veranda and headed home towards the P Section. As Mwila and I left the shops that day, I was in no doubt that the township would never be the same again.

Chapter 4

Jt was a night of interrupted sleep. The nightmares kept waking me up. Every time I closed my eyes, I fell into some sort of troubled sleep; I saw IFA trucks flashing lights, paramilitary officers firing tear gas canisters and fiery objects flying over my head. Windows were smashed. Mwila was shaking with fear. I was trying to look brave for her sake but was equally scared.

The noise I heard was not in my dreams. It was a rough bang on my door that knocked down the poster of Bob Marley from the wall. I jumped out of bed, steadied myself against the wall, and rescued my idol from the floor. Rubbing the sleep from my eyes, I heard the five AM alarm wailing. It was a routine. There was a change of shift at the underground mine.

"Lumba!" The voice startled me. Staggering through the living room, I found the door handle. With sleep still in my eyes, I turned the knob around and opened it.

"Where is Mwila?" He asked the moment he stormed in without sharing pleasantries.

"What do you mean? She is at her house," I said to Chisenga in amazement. He ignored my response and asked the same question, "Where is she?" I heard him but decided to ignore the issue. I pointed to a seat, but he did not take it. He paced about the room, and I left him alone and went to the shower.

"Where is Mwila?" he shouted from the living room once more.

"She is not here!" I shouted back. I extended my arm to the running water and retracted it instantly. A quick face wash would do. I used a wet face towel to wipe all the critical areas that needed it, and I was ready.

"Lumba, this is serious, she was not at home the whole afternoon," he said.

"Whose home?" I asked.

"Her family home was quiet. The doors were locked. I waited for a long time but could not stand the tear gas canisters, so I left," he ranted.

"I know. You must be tired; so why don't you sit down," I said, pushing a chair towards him.

The mine alarm was not wailing anymore. It was a relief. The night shift miners had been lifted successfully to the surface. If the siren had sounded for more than fifteen minutes, I would have worried. Everyone in the township would have been anxious. Women would not take their goods to sell at the market, and the children would miss school. Relatives of the injured would arrive from the village. As was usually the case, the house would be too small to host all the visiting villagers. Neighbours would offer their homes to accommodate visiting relatives. That's how mine townships functioned. It was a moral duty, and a traditional Zambian way of life and a socialism ideology of humanism the Republican President Kaunda espoused.

"Are you okay, Lumba?" I do not know whether he said it once or twice.

"Yeah, yeah, yeah. I am just tired," I said, standing up.

Immediately, I heard a vehicle close to my house.

"That does not sound like a mine vehicle, does it?" I said. It was a vain attempt to change the subject.

"Are you going to tell me where Mwila is?" Chisenga said impatiently.

I looked at the anxious Chisenga. His voice was sharp. I wondered why he had to come so early in the morning.

"Honestly, Chisenga, you don't think she slept here, do you?" I complained, strolling to the door and started aligning the picture of Bob Marley. Even without looking at his face, I could feel Chisenga's piercing look on my back.

Suddenly, a pain shot through my temples. I gave my forehead a gentle squeeze, but instead of going away, the hurt became a throbbing headache.

"You look exhausted," said Chisenga.

"I was resting, and you disturbed me!" All the piled-up stress bubbled up and consumed me.

"I did not plan to keep Mwila for that long. I told you we would be at Nkote Club after the game. It was all out of my control." I paused. Chisenga's eyes widened.

I resumed, "You introduced me to her, and now you are acting as if I took her away from you." I stopped myself and took a deep breath.

"Mwila is at her home; at least that's where I left her last night." I murmured thinking that was all the explanation I needed to give.

"I checked for her at nine o'clock last night, and she was

not there! What do you want me to think?" Chisenga said gravely, glancing around.

Then it dawned on me, Chisenga was showing genuine concern.

"I am sorry, Chisenga I thought you were trying to catch me out. I escorted her home and made sure she was inside and safe. That was about midnight. If it were not for the police and heavy rain, we would have been at her place before the mine siren went off at five o'clock yesterday afternoon," I explained.

Chisenga relaxed and picked up his massive raincoat and went for the door. "She is like my sister, and you know that. I am the only friend she has in the P Section."

"I know that, Chisenga." I shrugged, and I felt the tension in my muscles, and the throbbing in my head got worse.

I stared out of the window. It was still raining.

"Mwila's father is admitted at the J Clinic. I would not want to bring more miseries to her than what she already has." Chisenga paused, and we both turned towards the window. "Lumba, ever since Mwila came back from university, she has not been herself."

"I don't know what she's like, but she was alright with me, well, considering the bombardments of the paramilitary men."

I drew the curtains further apart.

"Did you walk in the shower? I enquired, watching the drops of rain.

Chisenga nodded, "I could not sleep, worrying about Mwila. Well, the rain is not that heavy," He said, looking at his raincoat.

"Shall we go and see Mwila?" said Chisenga, grabbing the raincoat. We headed for the door. It was still drizzling.

Chapter 5

*C*hisenga and I took the route by the shops on the way to Mwila's house. The clouds began to dissipate, and the sky became bright. It was a quiet gravel road littered with plastic bags and pieces of broken toys and heaps of mealie meal. We dodged carton boxes floating in the drainages and pools of water.

As we progressed in the street, I could feel that the sun was gaining strength, and in the distance, it formed a brilliant rainbow over the mineshaft. The colours of the rainbow were a welcome sight. Everyone in the compound believed a rainbow was a sign that the rains were over for the day.

We went past the houses that had *matambula*, mango and avocado trees. The sun cut through the leaves, and I felt the temperature rising. Soon, it shone brightly bringing with it the smell of warm earth. I loved the smell of the soil following the rain.

Along the street were anthills locally called *chulu*. Cracks appeared on them. We noticed the soil was giving in to a force coming from within it. Termites emerged through the cracks. They forced themselves out from inside the anthills and raptured on to the warm surroundings. We watched as the sun grew more prominent in the sky, and more cracks appeared on the *chulu*. The flying ants flew to freedom, spreading their wings in the direction of the sun.

Chisenga and I walked in the shadow of the swarms of the insects. It was a familiar sight that I had witnessed every rain season just before Christmas. The rain would fall and soften the soil and pave the way for insects to emerge from the earth below. The termites would fly away from the mounds, soaring over the compound. The reddish soil would warm up, releasing a distinct fragrance.

"Inswa! Inswa!" Children pushed the gates. Chisenga and I stopped to watch the children. With empty bottles of Coca-Cola and Fanta, the children raced up the mound. Settling down, they circled the cracks and trapped the insects.

"More here!"

"A big one here!"

"This one is struggling!"

Children picked their prey as they emerged.

"Inswa! Inswa!" The hill became a hive of pushing and shoving. Consequently, few insects emerged out of the holes. Some insects were unfortunate. Before they could make their getaway, the children snatched them by their heads and dropped them into the bottles that were filling up quickly.

The cracks became dark with black wings sprawling. Calls of, "I have got one!" and "I have got two" and "My bottle is full!" filled the air.

When I looked up the sky, the sun had risen above the wheels of the mineshaft. I felt we had wasted enough time watching children, but I could not leave, longing for more termites to fly to the sky.

"I have filled up two bottles!" said a boy with excitement.

"What are you going to do with the termites?" I asked.

"Take them home!"

"Sell them at the market!" answered another boy proud of his catch.

"Sell them to the women in the evening at Nkote Club." Said a girl with a full bottle.

"What would women do with *inswa*?" I inquired cheerfully.

"Dry them or fry them and sell them as snacks. Hum!" She rubbed her tummy. I also felt myself salivate. *Inswa* is a once a year delicacy.

"Mwila must have rested enough by now. Shall we go, Lumba?" Chisenga said.

"Oh, yes. We need to hurry now, Chisenga," I said.

We left the hill and went in the direction of the Nkote Club. The mist was lifting off the grass. It was so lovely watching the day unfold in the township, showing the beauty of the Savannah.

Above me, I heard the pure and sweet melodies of the birds. We watched birds chirping at each other and battling over *inswa*. The birds moved their heads from side to side like they had a switch in their brains that flicked to choose the direction of the prey. Every turn was rapid, almost too fast to see. They were singing with delight from the electrical wires, snapping up the flying termites wandering in the sky.

Eventually, Chisenga and I cut across the grass and stopped in front of a shop opposite the road. It was a tiny shop, brown bricks, with two large glass windows. The doors of Fyonse General Dealers were closed.

I was delighted to see Mr Phiri.

"Was the shop looted in yesterday's riots?" I asked. Mr Phiri shook his head.

Clearing his throat, he answered, "I don't know, Lumba. Yesterday, some young men threatened to loot."

"Are the men from this compound, Mr Phiri?" I asked.

Mr Phiri shook his head again, suppressing a cough. In some way, it seemed like a reflex action that removes foreign bodies from the airway. But then Mr Phiri made a whooping sound. I waited before I asked, "Are you having trouble to breathe?" He did not answer.

We stood in silence, looking inside the shop. Boxes containing clothes lay next to the sewing machine. The shelves looked disorderly. Books were piled on stacks of sugar, cooking oil containers lay on the mealie meal bags, pans of buns on top of empty crates of drinks. It was not something I had seen before.

"A woman accused a guy called Hector of looting the shop," I began to say.

Chisenga stared at me with a puzzled look and asked, "Who is Hector and who is this woman?"

Before I could respond, we were startled by an IFA lorry. Four paramilitary officers disembarked. Marching towards us, they shouted, "Stop!" I looked around the corridor.

"Planning to loot the shop?" said one of the officers. In between coughs, Mr Phiri said, "We are waiting for the shop to open. I am a tailor, and my Singer machine is inside the shop."

"There is no shop opening today. *Chokani!* (Leave!)" The military men commanded us in Nyanja.

We left the paramilitary men patrolling the veranda. Instinctively, I turned towards Nkote Club, and Chisenga followed me. "Where are you going?" Mr Phiri asked. "To see Mwila," I said.

Mr Phiri stood still, and said, "Mwila came to the shop yesterday. I have not seen her in a long time. Where has she been?"

"At University," said Chisenga.

"Alright," said Mr Phiri.

"I need to visit the forest. Can we go together, I will let you go to see Mwila after," he continued. We followed him at once, changing course towards Chamboli Market. Crossing the Lwanshimba Road, we stopped at the Milemu forest near the Kamatemate Stream.

Mr Phiri said as though to himself, "Right here, over thirty years ago, I planted a eucalyptus tree. I like coming over here to clear my lungs." Immediately, I understood what he meant. It was like *Vicks*. I took a deep breath of fresh air that ran through my lungs like a decongestant. Mr Phiri was not coughing any more. I took in the air continuously, and I wanted to sit on the roots and breathe freely. It was a calming and relaxing experience. I began to wonder what it would be like if the forests were to disappear entirely.

"Milemu forest was a campsite to the Central African Jamboree for the World Scout Association. Is that true?" asked Chisenga.

"I remember that well. It was in June 1952," answered Mr Phiri with a warm smile.

"Was that before you planted the eucalyptus trees?" I asked.

"Yes, Lumba," said Mr Phiri. "The name Chamboli comes from here. I blame my tribal cousins, the Bembas. They can not pronounce jamboree. They have no j and r on their tongues," he laughed.

"So, they came up with Chamboli," said Chisenga.

"It's a great name," I said, and we started to laugh, but Mr Phiri began to cough again. "Are you okay?" I asked. "I can feel the fresh aroma from the eucalyptus trees clearing my lungs," said Mr Phiri. I looked at Chisenga, and he just shrugged and said nothing.

"Where did the scouts come from?" I enquired.

"From the Northern Rhodesia as Zambia was known then. There were scouts from Nyasaland and Southern Rhodesia, Poland and the United Kingdom."

"Were they living in the compound?" I asked.

"Africans lived in the compound, and some still live here. The British, Americans, Poles and all Europeans lived on the other side of the mineshaft. During the war, the British brought the Poles in thousands and set up camp in Bwana Mkubwa not too far from here. However, most of them went back to Europe after the Second World War was over," he answered. His voice was confident.

"Did you fight in the Second World War?" I asked.

"No, Lumba. But I know from the patrons of the compound that miners worked night and day to dig up the copper for the British to make weapons and fight Hitler's German."

"Was the war like the riots of yesterday? Did you see a lot of *Mazembe* vehicles? Or *Caterpillars*? Were there a lot of mine tipper trucks carrying copper?" Chisenga asked without taking a breath.

"Yes, there were a lot of activities, but I am not sure about *Mazembe* or *Caterpillar.* Earth-moving vehicles have been roaming the Copperbelt as long as I have lived. Over ten per cent of all the copper used in the Second World War by the British came from this region."

Suddenly, the idea of the quantity of copper interested me. I looked at Mr Phiri and said, "That's a lot of copper!"

"There were too many wars going on. And the First World War ended right here in Zambia," Mr Phiri said. My eyes widened. I looked around as if I might see some remnants of the troops taking a forest cover!

"What got this region in a European war then?" asked Chisenga.

Mr Phiri looked over the anthills beyond the Milemu forest across the Kamatemate River. I turned my gaze to the big wheels spinning on the mineshaft. Smoke was rising from chimneys next to the mineshaft, and I heard the ventilation fan blowing the air from the underground tunnels. I turned and saw a military vehicle coming towards us.

I looked around. There was no route for motor vehicles in the forest—only a pathway made by the foot traffic connected Chamboli to Wusakile. The truck kept coming on the footpath, making the earth below my feet throb. I watched the giant tyres of the vehicle dig the soil underneath them.

Four paramilitary officers jumped out of the IFA. Looking at the ground, the insects were smashed and the roots bruised. I was beginning to wonder how long the forest would last. The police ordered us to go to our homes. Now, I was angry that I could not see Mwila.

Chapter 6

The morning was strangely calm, as the reddish sun rays shone brightly through the trees and warmed my face. Leaves and fruits dangled from the *matambula*, mango and pawpaw trees growing in my garden. The guava and avocado trees tossed in the wind at a house in front of mine. From the electric wire that connected the two homes, the birds flew to the mango tree. They sang like they had never seen a warm morning before.

Children waking up in their loud merrymaking disturbed my enjoyment of the music from the birds. The noise escalated as children chased chickens coming out of their shelters. And I was startled by a knock on the gate.

"Hello, Lumba."

"Hello, Mwila."

"I am going to the parish. I thought to pass through. Would you like to come with me?" I stared at Mwila.

"Yes," I said.

"So, the umbrella did not break?" I asked. She looked at it and flicked it open.

"It is a strong umbrella. And thanks for taking me to the football match and braving through the rain. It's a shame we did not see my father," Mwila said flatly. I felt like she was describing something that happened a long time ago.

"Oh, don't mention it! And thanks for coming along," I chirped.

"Have you been to the J Clinic?"

"Yes. My father is recovering." Mwila shifted her gaze to the floor, looked around my yard, and she forced a smile.

"That's good," I said. Not sure what else to say, I added, "Did you see any IFA trucks on your way here?"

"No military vehicles." She shook her head, anxiously. She seemed not to want to talk much. I could read her face now considering what Chisenga had said the previous day. "Possibly, she was not her normal self. But what was her usual self before she returned from university?" I wondered, wishing I had pressed Chisenga for more information.

"I am going now to the parish. See you there, Lumba!" she shouted and hastened to the gate. "See you soon, Mwila." I grinned as my eyes followed her. She crossed the Kalukungu Road and disappeared in the L Section.

The birds were still singing, and children ran up and down the yards.

"*Mwashibukeni!* (Good morning!)." Families were waking up and sharing greetings.

"*Eya mukwai!* (We are fine and thank you!)" sounded around the neighbourhood. I smelt the ooze of burning braziers. There were conversations about the riots and the ordination of the priests at the parish.

"Where were you when the tear gas canisters began to explode?" one asked.

"I was visiting a friend!" they answered.

"Are you going to the parish?"

"Yes!"

"Maybe!"

And then I watched a man riding his bicycle with a load of charcoal. I guessed he was going to the Chamboli Market. A yellow Toyota truck marked F23 passed by me. Personal belongings of a family shifting from one section of the mine compound to another filled up the mine vehicle. More yellow mine vans and lorries rumbled on the Kalukungu Road.

I weaved through the crowds shopping for Christmas, and a "Happy New Year, Happy Christmas" song reverberated around the shops. Edging through the dense flow of people with bags and basket full of supplies, I watched the Jamas Milling and Chimanga Changa Milling trucks off-loading mealie-meal bags into the Zambia Consumer Buying Corporation (ZCBC) Stores. I pushed and shoved to get through foot traffic swerving delivery vans. George Bakery. Supaloaf. Copperbelt Bottlers. It was a long queue of commercial lorries and vans.

When I finally crossed the road, I looked back at the many people that crowded the shops. I followed a crowd through the L Section. There were a lot of houses which had flower gardens. Without traces of broken fences or litter, I wondered if the riots and explosions had reached this side of the compound. And then I recalled the residents of Chamboli liked to sweep the houses and the yards each morning and afternoon. With the music blasting from houses, I had a feeling the compound was back to itself.

I strode through the crowded residential street. The

bongo-drummed music thumped from the direction of the parish, getting louder as I got closer to the churchyard.

Arriving at the parish, I saw tents standing in the open ground. I had never seen so many shelters. I knew Father Katyetye was popular in the compound. "The parishioners must have assisted him," I thought. I spotted Catholic worshippers. Women wore green chitenge materials printed with praying hands. When I saw men and women picking up litter from the grounds, I realised the riots had affected the parish too. They were gathering rubbish in one pile. I joined a group of youths who were mending a fence.

"Do you know Mwila?" I asked the one who seemed to be the leader.

"Mwila who? Which Mwila?" she answered. It dawned on me I did not know her surname.

"Mwila from the P Section," I said.

"I do not know Mwila from the P Section."

I began to describe, but the woman stopped me. "You have to look for her yourself."

A noisy engine made me turn in the direction of the entrance—military vehicles were parking at the gate of the parish. Immediately, I shifted my gaze to the leader who was now wearing a puzzled look. "What are they doing here?" she said, pointing to the entrance.

"Providing security," I said in jest. The catholic young woman did not take the joke. She narrowed her eyes and said, "The house of God does not need the security of men. The Lord will take care of us."

"God uses ordinary men to guard his people," I said slowly to show conviction.

"Not the men that have destroyed his house. Look at the fence," she said gesturing.

"Did they do that?" I asked, looking around.

"It took us three years to be ready, and they destroyed it in one day." The woman said, waving her hands to show the destruction.

"They were chasing people that looted the shops and stole mealie meal bags," I explained, attracting her intense stare.

"Are they looking for the looters here?" she said.

"I can ask the driver," I said when I saw the church van stop at the entrance. The driver took his time to pass the gate. He was talking to the paramilitary officers.

"I will wait for the driver to leave the entrance," I added.

We waited, but the Catholic lady did not have the perseverance of the saints. "I must keep to the work of the Lord, and you keep seeking for your friend," she said and walked away. I glanced around. Mwila was not anywhere in sight.

A little later, the church van entered the churchyard. "Hello, Peter!" I called following a Pickup van. Peter did not answer. Instead, he drove on and parked his van near the hedge.

"Peter! What do the paramilitary officers want?" I asked calmly, but he did not answer, and I began to doubt if Peter had heard me. Walking close to him, I asked Peter the same question. He looked at me with a blank face. I was not getting any word from him.

Annoyed, I turned back and followed his passengers who were disappearing in the thick crowd of worshippers.

I thrilled at the sight of the regalia and piety revealing the new arrivals were from other Copperbelt towns; Ndola, Luanshya, Mufulira, Chingola, Kalulushi and Chililabombwe.

Pushing through the parishioners, I spotted Father Katyetye in front of a delegation of the clergy strolling towards the podium. The churchyard began to overflow, and I was mystified by the smell of the incense that blew everywhere.

"Here you are!" I turned around, and Mwila was holding my hand and gestured, "Follow me," she said urgently through trembling lips.

"Have you found a better place than this one?" I asked.

"Please, Lumba, follow me. Quickly!" I noticed she was nervous, but I was not sure why.

"Where are we going?"

The corridor led into a hallway which had carton boxes stuck on the side of the wall. The smell was that of old books. Hymn books and pamphlets piled up into a church library. Mwila turned her back on me and advanced down the library. I walked briskly to catch up with her. She was walking too fast, almost running. "Close the door behind you!" she said without looking back.

"The ordination has started, Mwila. Where are we going?"

"Please, Lumba, close the door." I turned back, closing the door gently. Walking faster than before, I stumbled over the steps. I decided to be silent and stayed a few steps behind Mwila. Then she turned into a hallway which was not well lit. There was no natural light, and candles were burning dimly. The bookshelves along the corridor were up to the ceiling. More books appeared, and I stopped when I saw covers that were separate from the books. Stepping towards me, Mwila got my hand to go.

Eventually, the dim aisle opened into a small room. The sign on the door revealed the "Music Room." Mwila did not let go of my hand, and for that reason, we struggled to walk. We bumped into furniture. Tables. Drums. Chairs. Piano. Then I began to hear voices. They were coming from a room ahead of us. I stalled.

"That's where we are going," said Mwila urging me to move.

"What's going on, Mwila?" I said again.

"People are talking," she said.

"Talking about what?" I asked in a worried tone.

The doors of the "Prayer Room" opened suddenly. Mwila stood near the door. She looked like a guard controlling traffic in and out of a secured emerald or copper mine area. I stood behind her, afraid to be seen by the occupants we found.

Then a man said, "Now, Micky, are you going to say something?" The room went quiet.

"Six months ago, the Chief Mine Captain of Mukuba Mining Corporation was in the compound," said Micky.

"Where in the township?" enquired another man in a deep voice.

"Near the market. And had we not known the registration number for the mine vehicle, we would not have noticed the Chief Mine Captain. The car stopped near my stall, and there I saw the Chief. He was talking with the Honourable MP," said Micky. He continued, "We stood near the car for a good while watching the two men pointing fingers at each other. They disagreed about everything — the miners' salaries, the redundancies and the minerals. The Chief said, 'Copper does not grow on the mine as mangoes do in the compound. It is a wasting asset, and there isn't much of it left underground anymore.'"

I looked at Mwila and wondered if she understood everything that was going on. Her face was calm, and I decided she understood everything.

Micky took off the dark glasses and his hat to expose a handsome youthful face. Wiping his brow with the hat, he put the glasses back on and cleared his throat. He spoke like he was addressing a rally of mineworkers. "The Chief Mine Captain was tapping on the sheets of paper saying, 'Numbers do not lie. Mukuba Mining Corporation is making losses.'"

There was silence. I watched the attentive faces in the room. Everyone was facing Micky. "Now listen, Champions," said Micky, "I am telling you the mine makes money. The company exports minerals every day and sends money overseas. Since the company has become stingy and does not maintain the roads, houses or any facilities in our compound anymore, we cannot trust it. They promised investment in production. But it is not here, and as a result, no new jobs." He paused, looking around, and forcing a smile. Clearing his throat, he continued, "All that time in the car, the honourable member of parliament kept saying, 'The government does not have money. Why? Loans. The cold-blooded monsters are squeezing the hand of government.'" Micky paused for effect.

"Who are these monsters?" yelled someone.

"The International Monetary Fund," said Micky.

"It is not me speaking. The MP said it," he added.

"So, Buteko blames the IMF and not the mine?"

"Buteko heaped it on the mine too. Mukuba Mining Corporation is not paying enough taxes forcing the government to borrow. Now the IMF is charging colossal amounts in interest rates."

"About grants?"

"The cold beast is surviving on struggling economies. Buteko's words, not mine," said Micky shaking his head.

He stood up, hit his fist on his chest, and said in a voice full of pain, "When I heard that, I knew, and God knew no one was interested in our township."

There was silence. Then Micky removed his glasses again, and his gaze met mine, and he said, "We must act now. The Chief Mine Captain does not care about us." He looked around the room and lowered his voice, "The mining company is selling the stadium!"

There were startled gasps of pain. Everyone stood up, walking about the room and punching the fists in the air. Mwila pushed me aside, slammed the door behind me, leaving me exposed to all the occupants. I moved towards the door and leaned against it. Then the wall clock buzzed. It was two PM. I watched the nervous gaze of the men, which frightened me. I moved slightly from the door when Micky pointed at me, "Is he your friend?" Mwila nodded.

I could hear my heartbeat as my mind wondered whether Mwila was someone I could trust. I told myself to get out, or I would be punching clenched fists in the air when I had no idea what this was all about. Micky was still looking at me. My eyes were on the pieces of prayer requests pinned behind him.

I scanned for the door handle, feeling it on my back. Mwila moved towards me, judging my intentions. She turned the doorknob, grabbed my arm, and pulled me out of the prayer room. Then she shut the door behind her, and we stood outside facing each other.

"Lumba, can you do me a favour?" she said her lips trembling. She closed her eyes for a moment, sighed deeply, and opened her eyes. She was staring at me.

I shrugged, "Depends on what it is."

"Do you believe the mining company is to blame?" she asked and looked away from me.

"Blame for what, Mwila?"

Mwila looked down. Then she said, "You heard them. They blame it on the mining corporation." She turned around and began to walk away. I followed her through the winding church hall corridors. We emerged out of the building to the open fields.

"There!" Mwila pointed me towards a fence. She started speaking in whispers as she led me away.

"Where are we going?" I asked in a whisper as well.

She did not answer. Hurriedly, she pulled me along the edge of the churchyard. And in a sudden motion, she stopped and began to examine a plant.

"There!" she whispered.

"Where?".

She did not take off her eyes from the potted plant.

"There!" she repeated, her hand firmly pointing to the hedge. "There, behind the potted plant. I will get the market vendors through there."

"Which market vendors?" I asked.

"Micky and…." She paused, looked around, began to

lower herself and stopped mid-way. I turned around and saw no one watching us. The faithful Catholics and their visitors were engaged in prayers. Mwila's face seemed calm. She knelt on the ground. Pushing the big potted plant aside, she revealed a hole in the *lunsonga* hedge. At that moment, her peaceful face turned into terror. She looked horrified at what she was doing.

"What now?" I asked.

She was silent, staring at the hole. She got up and put her palms together in a gesture of prayer. "Follow me," she said and held my hand, leading me on like a child. We walked swiftly in the crowd and stopped at the corner of the church library.

She made the sign of praying hands again.

"Stay here, Lumba," she said. Her voice was sharp and commanding.

"What for?"

"All you have to do is watch for the paramilitary police. If the police come this way, put your hands together as if in prayer."

I was terrified. "Why are you doing this?"

"The market vendors are saving the minerals from plunder."

"I do not know about that," I said.

"Lumba, listen. The mining company is selling assets. The Chief Mine Captain is selling the stadium. The mining company does not care about us. They will take over the emerald mines as well," she concluded stroking my arm. It did the trick and calmed me down. I took a deep breath.

"Did the men in the Prayer Room loot the Chimanga Changa maize meal lorry?"

"No," she said as she walked away and disappeared in the crowd. I looked around but could not see her.

Standing next to me, two men talked about their faith. "The only way to salvation is through Christ. Not through the priests," one said.

"Things have changed," said the other man. "Now, people can read the bibles for themselves and salvation through Christ has taken a firm hold."

I was digesting this information when I looked at the entrance. I counted three IFA trucks and a contingent of paramilitary officers. They were talking to people going out and coming in.

For a brief moment, I moved my gaze to worshipers prostrating on the ground. With so many faithful Christian followers, I wondered why God did not spare the township, let alone the parish.

"Vroom." The sound jolted me to gaze at the main gate where two more IFA trucks were parking and military officers, armed in riot gear, were jumping from the vehicles. They lined up at the entrance, and any minute, they would be storming the parish. When I looked in the direction of the Church Library, I noticed that the door was closed. "Where is Mwila?" I put my hands together as if I was saying a prayer, and shortly after, I felt a tap on my shoulder.

"Thank you." It was Mwila.

"They have gone, Lumba," she added.

"Why did you do that?"

"I told you...the mining company is selling the stadium, and they are going to take over the emerald mines. We need to..." She paused.

"Act now?" I said.

"Yes, together. You and me, we need to save the township," Mwila said coolly.

I shook my head, and she shrugged her shoulders.

Standing side by side, Mwila and I talked in jumbled whispers. We frequently looked over our shoulders and at the entrance of the churchyard. We tried hard to enjoy the ordination. People were singing and dancing. The jubilations and laughter seemed infectious, but somehow, the two of us failed to catch the spirit.

"The mining company does not care about us, Lumba," she said with a nervous smile.

"The minerals have become a problem for the compound, Lumba," Mwila added.

"What do we do about that?" I asked, and the feeling of hopelessness made me jittery.

"There's no turning back," she replied almost at once.

My heart skipped a beat.

"What have we done? What have I done?" I wondered, feeling trapped without a way out. If there was a way out, then I did not see it. I staggered and stumbled and bumped into the congregants.

"I need some water," I said more to myself than to Mwila.

I shook my head to clear my mind. It seemed to me that I needed space more than I needed water: Space to breathe: Space away from Mwila. I looked behind, and there she was.

"Are you okay?" Mwila asked. I ignored her and turned the water tap on, cupped my hands and gulped down some fresh, soothing water.

We moved away from the tap towards the podium. In an instant, Father Katyetye's solemn prayer silenced the conversations. Every word was like he was addressing Mwila and me. "Confess your sins to the Lord and let Him cleanse you. Come to the Lord as you are." The sensation of guilt came over me. Somehow God had told the priest to bring us to confession.

I covered my ears when I began to hear tear gas explosions. The face of the baby that almost choked to death flashed before me. I felt my head was spinning. I strove to block the voices in my head, but they kept on coming. The memories of the broken fence behind the potted plants made it worse.

I was staggering towards the entrance. My heart was beating hard. When I got to the gate, I was trembling with anxiety, holding my breath as I passed the policemen. But Mwila did not look bothered.

Chapter 7

I felt the sun was beginning to lose its bright orange colour quickly, and there was a cold breeze blowing. Mwila and I walked in silence for what seemed a long time on the sparsely populated township roads. Living in Chamboli meant people would be out and about in the evening, but it was quiet. Somewhere in the distance, I could hear an owl hooting. I felt like the darkness was falling fast. But Mwila walked seemingly confidently, undisturbed by the darkness. "Only a few nights ago, she was running scared of darkness," I thought.

We turned a corner at the bus stop to join the Kalukungu Road. From the end of the street, a pair of headlights came bouncing over. I knew right away; it was not a mine vehicle. All the mine vehicles, including the F23 truck, stopped moving by 5 PM. So, when the IFA truck passed us, rumbling along the road, I was not surprised it was a military vehicle. Still, I was scared of seeing the military police in riot gears. The indicators revealed the truck was going towards the parish.

I could feel Mwila's eyes were looking at me. But I did not want to look at her. And I did not want to think about the parish. So I focussed through the darkness of the night, plodding forward, feet wallowing in the wet pools from the downpour of previous days.

"Lumba, the shops are still open!" said Mwila, pointing at Fyonse General Dealers. The fluorescent tubes lit on the shop corridor. Mwila paused on the road, letting her eyes roam the shop corridors while surveying my actions. She seemed aware that I wanted to be left alone. So, she spent a few minutes longer to wait for my decision. In my frozen state, I let out a shaky breath. I felt like emerging from the anger that possessed me.

"Why is it open this time of the evening?" I said, controlling my voice. Mwila did not answer. Instead, she started walking towards the shop. I turned and followed her.

On the corridor near the entrance stood a box full of clothes. Between the cartons was a Singer sewing machine. The chair and radio revealed Mr Phiri was still working. Just as we arrived, Mr Phiri came from inside the shop and got to work on his sewing machine.

"Hello, Mr Phiri," said Mwila, a bit jovial for my liking.

"Hello, Mwila. Hello, Lumba," said Mr Phiri.

"A lot of clothes today," said Mwila pointing at clothes hanging on the grill doors and in the boxes.

"They have piled up. I could not get the sewing machine out. The shop did not open yesterday."

"Riots?" she asked. I watched her powerlessly as she spoke seemingly very innocent.

"Yes, everyone is talking about them," responded Mr Phiri, "Shop owners are nervous. How's your father?"

Mwila narrowed her eyes and said, "He's fine. He was asleep all the time when I visited him last time. I think he is improving. I promised myself to revisit him since I had no chance to talk to him the last time." She looked in my direction. I nodded like a coward and looked away from her, inspecting windows.

"How long am I going to be quiet about the parish? Is this going to become some secrete?" I wondered.

I noticed there were burglar bars over the two large glass display windows. "Got fitted today?" I asked Mr Phiri, desperately to disrupt Mwila's questions.

"Yes, they have been fitted to protect the glass doors. Have you seen the notice here?" he said, pointing. "The honourable member of parliament has hired Zempya Security guards and fitted the alarms," he said, and I nodded.

Then, the sound of a noisy engine made us turn towards the Kalukungu Road. IFA lorries were rumbling on the way. I knew the destination but did not want to think about it.

"He is lucky the mine still employs him, and he can get his treatment," said Mr Phiri returning to the topic of Mwila's sick father. Mwila shook her head. She seemed agitated. "Everything okay, Mwila?" said Mr Phiri.

"I volunteered to be an usher at the ordination," She began to say, her lips trembling. "I was welcoming the visitors to the parish and finding them places where they could worship comfortably. As I walked about, I heard raised voices from the library." Mwila turned and met my gaze. I pretended like I knew that to be true.

"I went in and found men discussing." She shook her head.

"Sit down," said Mr Phiri pulling two stools from under the heap of clothes.

"I can see the shelves in the shops are now full. There were a lot of delivery trucks. ROP. Vitafoam. National Milling. Lyons Brookebond. Mansa Batteries." I was desperate to change the subject. I did not want to think about what had happened at the parish. I was afraid. I was guilty.

"I do not think all the shops got their orders. Patel did not receive anything. He's not too happy. The shops are still facing shortages of commodities," said Mr Phiri.

There was a brief silence, but deep enough to oppress me. I could not think of what to fill the void. Then Mr Phiri asked, "What were the men at the parish talking about?"

"A mine strike," said Mwila, and she looked at me. I knew she was lying, but I said nothing.

"Mineworker's union call for meetings at the Milemu forest before instigating a strike. If this were a mine strike, the news would have circulated already. What's the nature of their grievance?" he asked.

"I don't know," she said. I knew she was lying again.

"That is not good. Union leaders don't hide their grievances. They stand by their decision. When votes came in to strike, we all know the issues very well."

"What issues concern union leaders?" asked Mwila.

"Miners' strikes are as old as the compound. We have had them since the colonial era when the British arrived and subjected this region to political control for their economic gain."

Mwila nodded and moved closer to Mr Phiri latching on the economic gain idea, "What do you mean for their economic gain? Is this the same thing happening now? The mining company controlling everything for their gain?" Mwila asked questions in succession. I noticed her excitement.

"The British took over the minerals by signing questionable treaties with chiefs. They hired private companies that did their dirty work for them, subjecting native miners to harsh conditions. It was not uncommon for the native miners to revolt. Have you been taught about John Cecil Rhodes, the British South African Company and the Anglo-American Corporation?"

"Yes," Mwila and I said in a chorus. I felt like I shook the tension out of my shoulders. Mr Phiri nodded. Suddenly, the night birds began to call. Insects of the night were hanging around the fluorescent tubes, and the shop received no visitors. I thought it was time for Mwila and me to leave, but she kept asking, and Mr Phiri seemed happy to respond.

"Copper brought the Anglo-Americans to the Lamba land and led them to build the township. Clinics. Stadium. Roads. Libraries." Then he paused and said, "But it was all from the copper they mined from this land."

I was attentive, judging every question Mwila asked.

"Good," she said unconvincingly.

"You look distracted. What is the matter, Mwila?" said Mr Phiri.

"The men at the library... They needed help... They talked angrily about the injustices of the mines." Mwila looked in my direction. I stared at her. She continued, "They were angry. Reductions of employees, the sale of the properties, the lack of maintenance of the township. That sort of thing."

As Mwila was talking, I heard a noise from behind

me. We all turned in the direction of the Asian Shopping Store. At the end of the corridor strolled a large man. His hands were on the tangling canisters around his waist. For a moment I thought he was about to throw a canister at us. Instead, he pulled out a long black baton from the side of his military trousers. I stood up when he stopped near me.

I noticed his shirt was too tight on the waist, and the buttons were almost popping out. His height matched mine, though he looked slightly taller due to the high laced heavy boots. He stepped towards me, and I could hear him breathing hard. I began to worry. He stared at Mwila, and then he turned his large dark eyes to me. "Good...Good... Good evening Mr Phiri." He stammered. His voice was hoarse.

"Good evening, PC Mambwe," said Mr Phiri.

"Working long hours?" asked PC Mambwe, pacing the floor of the veranda.

"Yes, to clear off a backlog," responded Mr Phiri coolly.

PC Mambwe squared his shoulders, swung his baton and moved again towards me. He pulled up his bulged trousers and rolled up his sleeves. The shade of his green striped uniform revealed he was from Kamfinsa Mobile Unit. He hung the baton on the belt around his waist and then rested his hand on his stomach. "Has the guard from Zempya arrived yet?" he growled in a deep, menacing voice.

"Not seen him around," said Mr Phiri.

"I am coordinating security. Can you tell the guard to find me at the parish entrance?"

My stomach churned. PC Mambwe was at the St. Michael & Noah's parish. "Could he have seen us pass?" I wondered.

"I will. If the guard turns up in time," Mr Phiri answered.

PC Mambwe marched down the corridor. Teargas canisters were swinging from side to side around his waist. He looked back at us, hesitated, and then resumed his journey in the direction of the parish.

Mwila sighed heavily. "Coordinating security? What does that mean?" asked Mwila looking anxious.

"He is looking for market vendors," said Mr Phiri. Mwila met my gaze.

"PC Mambwe was here three hours ago," Mr Phiri pointed at the spot where Mwila was, "He is after the men who started the looting. He said they sell cooking oil at the market." A moment passed, and no one spoke any word. Mwila shuffled her feet back and forth.

Chapter 8

J discovered the unpleasant reality of Mwila. She was manipulative, and I found myself with limited options. I was nervous about embarking on a journey that might never end. I resisted, but Mwila did not give up on this trip. And it was me that gave in. In return, she offered Chisenga, who knew nothing of her guilt.

"What is this plan of going to the emerald minefield?" Chisenga gave me a blank expression.

"I have no idea Chisenga. I do not know what she wants. You know her better than I do," I said with exasperation in my tone.

The clock on my wall showed five o'clock in the morning, and I could hear the mine alarm wailing.

"Give me an honest answer, Lumba. Did you go on a date again?" asked Chisenga.

"No. Are you kidding?" I said.

"What were you doing at the parish together then?" he said.

I closed my eyes, and I said; "I hope it is just my imagination, but she appears extraordinarily unpredictable. I have just known her for a week, but it feels like a year.

57

Strangely, I feel very protective of her." I paused and opened my eyes. Chisenga gave me a sympathetic look.

"I also feel a bit confused. But here we are deep into whatever Mwila is up to. It is like we are a couple of sympathetic fools," Chisenga said as we shook our heads at the same time.

"Has she always been this strange?" I asked. Chisenga was silent, and I realised the alarm at the mineshaft had stopped ringing. It was now ten minutes past five, and the only noise I could hear was the ventilation fans from the M Section.

"We are late. Mwila is waiting for us." I said in a panic. Chisenga tied a bottle of water to the back of the bicycle seat. The string was a rubber band from a used tube of a bicycle tyre. Jumping on the bicycle, Chisenga pedalled away as I held on to the saddle from the carrier.

On the way, behind the brown brick shops of Fyonse General Dealers and Asian Shopping Store, the dim, cold dawn was quiet. The cold air of the rainy morning was stiffening our faces. I did not see a single mine-vehicle. After riding for a while, we began to meet market vendors, men, and women, carrying bags of food supplies to Chamboli Market. We rode through the dark gravel roads until Chisenga detoured and joined the Kalukungu Road. A file of mine bicycles was rumbling along the street. The miners were talking noisily together as they headed towards the underground mine.

When our eyes started to itch, I thought of only one thing. "Tear gas canisters."

Chisenga disagreed. "No, Lumba, I can smell *Senta*."

"*Senta* in the morning?" I despaired.

"Mukuba Mining Corporation has increased the production of copper," said Chisenga.

"It is strange that the mining company could be releasing *Senta* early in the morning instead of the usual afternoon. The township people could suffocate in their sleep," I responded.

"The smelters have increased emissions at night," said Chisenga.

"So that residents do not notice?" I asked.

"It is to protect the residents as they are assumed to be indoors."

"We are not indoors, Chisenga."

"I know that, Lumba."

The conversation was short-lived. As we emerged at Nkote Club, a bright light shone ahead of us. "Stop!" I shouted. Chisenga brought the bicycle to a halt a few meters away from an IFA truck. I wondered whether to jump off the bike and let on a sprint like Samuel Matete. I gave up the thought.

A stout police officer with a large potbelly jumped off the IFA truck. He pulled a baton from his waist and pointed it at me. Then he did the same with Chisenga. I recognised PC Mambwe, but then it was too late to tell Chisenga who our tormentor was. So I pretended I had never seen him before.

"Where are you going so early in the morning?" PC Mambwe looked at his watch.

"Going home," said Chisenga.

"We are not going home," I wanted to say, but I did not see a good reason to contradict Chisenga.

PC Mambwe walked forcefully around the bicycle.

"Where did you get the bicycle from?"

"Got it from my father. It was a free bicycle for twenty

years of continuous service with the mines," said Chisenga confidently. The police officer pointed the baton on the bicycle frame.

"Where does it say Mukuba Mining Corporation? I can only read Eagle on the frame. Have you got a receipt?" PC Mambwe growled. There was a part in me that did not trust this officer. I did not want to attract attention to myself. So, I left it all to Chisenga to answer the questions and deal with him.

"I don't know where the receipt is," responded Chisenga. The military man took out a little book and a pen.

"Your name?" PC Mambwe asked.

"Chisenga Waluse"

"You?"

"Lumba Chuma"

He scribbled our names in his little book. My gaze was on the baton that now hung on his belt. As he moved about, the teargas canisters tossed to and from his waist.

"Okay. You can go!"

Chisenga pushed the bicycle away in a hurry, and we quickly jumped on it. Without looking back, he picked up speed and pedalled harder.

It did not take long to find Mwila's house. A latch secured the gate, but Chisenga knew how to release it. Opening the gate, Chisenga led the way to the house. The red slab on the door entrance was highly polished, and I could smell *Cobra* wax floor polish, a popular brand in the township. On the floor was a rag of rectangular pieces of old colourful clothes woven on to an empty sack of Chimanga Changa bag. It was the kind of artistry made by women, from things that had no further use. It was not a skill that I could associate with Mwila, a temperamental young woman.

Chisenga's knock at the door attracted barks from the dogs. I looked around scared, not knowing who would answer our knock. On the second knock, the door opened. It was Mwila. Immediately, she smiled and shook hands with Chisenga. I crossed my arms, unimpressed with her. Then she paused before me. I thought she resisted the instinct to shake hands with me, and I thought to myself, "This girl is so unpredictable."

Here, now on the bike ready to go, and I was nervous. Before we rode forth, in search of what Mwila's adventure would bring, Chisenga briefed her. "There is an IFA truck at Nkote Club, isn't that so, Lumba?" I nodded.

"Did the police see you?" Mwila asked.

"They flushed the lights, and we stopped. One of them came and wanted to take the bicycle from us," answered Chisenga.

"It was PC Mambwe," I added, reluctantly. Mwila looked at me with bewilderment. "Why?" she asked.

"I guess the policeman thought it's a product of the loot!" I said.

"Are you sure it was PC Mambwe?" she asked.

"Slightly taller than I am, buttons on his shirt were almost popping out. He spoke Nyanja, stammers a bit..."

"Yes, that's him. That is PC Mambwe," cut in Mwila before Chisenga could finish his description. "He is coordinating security in the mine compound," Mwila added.

"What security?" asked Chisenga.

I realised Mwila had not briefed Chisenga on everything. I did not know if Chisenga knew all that happened at the parish and on the shop verandas.

Chapter 9

*M*wila explained the route in detail. Chisenga nodded as he directed the bicycle.

"I know the route," Chisenga reassured us.

"Avoid the main roads," said Mwila.

"But the *Santi* roads are too dark," said Chisenga.

"Okay, we can use the main road," retracted Mwila.

"What if we come across the IFA trucks?" I asked.

"We will figure out what to say," said Mwila.

We passed Mwabonwa Tavern and followed Natolo Street. The road rose a little between Bupe Primary School and the Nazarene Church. Turning towards the bus stop, we travelled on an unnamed *santi* road in the L Section. There were more unnamed roads than the named ones.

The residential areas appeared and disappeared one by one. We rode past the parish entrance, and it was quite. There were no IFA trucks stationed at the parish. I thought the paramilitary police had realised the men they came for had escaped. I wondered if they knew the market vendors had been helped by the girl that sat at the back of the Eagle.

Leaving the parish behind, we continued our journey through the M Section. The noise from the ventilation fans was deafening. Particles were rising from the vents blowing toxic dust and gases from the mine underground.

Soon the residential areas were far behind us, and we were in a thick bush. Chisenga cycled on the edge of defunct mine sites known by the locals as *ifilongoma*.

"Is this the safest route we could use?" I asked.

In response, Chisenga said, "Mr Phiri told us Anglo-American Corporation excavated the grounds and exploited them for Rhodes BSA company."

"And abandoned the excavations so close to the compound," I said.

"Mukuba Mining Corporation has continued the explorations and mining. They will abandon the current mine unsafely," said Mwila. Her voice was harsh.

Chisenga was now more focussed. He silently pedalled, controlling the wheels on the narrow path between *ifilongoma*. I looked on the sides in despair. There was no helping for the sick feeling in my stomach.

Then, I saw a warning sign. The area was out of bounds. "Mukuba Mining reserves the right to explore the rocks for mining," Mwila read the caution loudly and exhaled slowly. I did not like her tone at all.

I turned my attention to Chisenga as he was guiding the bicycle cautiously on the rugged road. We rode deep in silence. The small, loose stones reverberated around the wheels like a cymbal. I could feel the fear in my chest, waiting to take over. If we were to slip and fall, we would tumble and scream, through the godless pit and lost for all of eternity.

Countless times, I had heard stories about what lay in the bush near Chamboli. Some were tales of excavations with endless echoes. Others talked about voices muted by dams surrounded by heaps upon heaps of sand. They were journeys that crossed the Chibuluma River to Sailashi through small and broad roads.

There were certain areas away in the woodlands regarded as sacred for the mining explorations, and the mining company felt insulted and outraged if a resident were to trespass. When residents were unlucky and ran into the *Kanyangus*, the mine police sirens chased the invaders from the mine reserves. Bicycle bells rang, and dust rose. I never experienced any of this. But now, I was nervous. Anytime soon, we would be ducking in the woodlands away from the mine police units. And only if we made it alive through the pits.

Then impact. Everything was a blur, a blur that swirled out of existence. Suspended in the air, I closed my eyes and surrendered myself into the bottomless pit below. We were falling, down and down as I held Chisenga's hands on the handlebars. I opened my eyes to the rocks. They were darkening as if night came in seconds. And then a sigh of relief as we hang to a bush. "Thank God!" we screamed almost in unison. Looking down, I saw abandoned earth-moving equipment lay on the floor.

The time we spent pushing the bike from the depression lasted far longer than I had expected. I cursed the Anglo-American company for abandoning these sites without burying them. Eventually, we reached the top of the excavation, and I noticed the safety ropes were missing from the steel rods.

"The mining company should have filled up the

dangerous pits and not leave dangling ropes," I murmured. Mwila and Chisenga turned to me without a word.

For a short while, we did not ride on the bicycle preferring to roll it carefully in case of any more dangerous quarries. Eventually, we came to the end of the area. We now had to deal with safety ropes that barred our way. I wondered how we were going to cross that. Chisenga stooped down and crawled under them. After which, I lifted the bike over the ropes, and Chisenga received and lowered it on the other side. Then, Mwila and I crept under the strings, joining Chisenga on the other side.

Getting back on the bicycle, we rode through an area of tall trees, thick bushes, overhanging branches, and creeping plants. Gradually, the day started to get bright, and the warning messages were a lot clearer; Danger—explosives, Danger—Unsecured deeps. Danger — We will prosecute anyone apprehended beyond this point.

I resigned to the feeling that the journey that lay before us was peril on peril. There was no safe way through the bush Cecil Rhodes hired men ploughed through. Even if we made it through going, we had a return trip to worry about. And whatever reason or reasons Mwila wanted this trip for, I hoped it was bigger than the abandoned pits that were hungry to swallow us. And I was fully aware that if we got arrested, my casual work at the mine would terminate, the jobs of our parents would end too.

"Are we going in the right direction?" I asked. My question dangled in the air for a while longer. It was understandable for Chisenga not to answer. He needed to concentrate on riding the bike, but I was sceptical why Mwila was mute. She did not want to hear anything to question the trip. It was a journey only she knew where and why we were going. Her story to me was sketchy. "Lumba, who do you believe?" was what she had told me before. The next thing, she was proposing the trip. Why should I have had to choose between Micky and Mukuba Mining Corporation? It did not make sense to me. "Lumba, trust me!" she told me time and time again until I agreed to the trip.

I looked at poor Chisenga holding the handlebars directing the bicycle to the place he knew little of. At least that's what I thought. How could he possibly know the area when he was asking Mwila at every turn. "Should I turn left?" Chisenga would ask. "No, Chisenga. Turn right," Mwila would reply.

Eventually, we began to follow a narrow path covered in thick morning dew. We broke through the thatch of branches and leaves blocking most of the sun. The day was brightening more. In the distance, we heard a noise, and Chisenga slowed down the bike. Our eyes searched, watched, and waited for movements in the underbrush. Passing the bush, we looked down and saw little birds beaks of polished amber, hopping through longer shaggy grass, tugging at worms. I could not tell what Chisenga and Mwila thought of the scene. I tried to image a more excellent place for such specifies. And I could not think of any rich woodlands and grasslands to offer the birds such a natural home of cosiness and warmth.

I smiled, remembering the old adventures when we came back triumphant. We had caught birds with slimy glue-like *bulimbo* or knocked them down with homemade catapults. There were days too of stomach upsets from eating wild fruits on pricky branches or overgrowth; *masalampata*, *masafwa* or *intungulu*. Legends had it that township people got lost or vanished in thin air picking *intungulu*. As such, we learnt never to venture alone or pick *intungulu* with both hands.

"Can you see how beautifully the birds perch on the bushes and worms?" I said aloud. Chisenga nodded, but Mwila was silent.

Shortly afterwards, Mwila said, "Have you seen that lovely anthill." Both Chisenga and I turned to look at what she was pointing at. Indeed it had an unusual shape. It looked like the shape of an igloo. I wouldn't have called it a *chulu*; it was more like a gigantic termite mound. "I need a break. Maybe we can have a look at it." Chisenga stopped his Eagle bicycle. Trotting over the grass, we came close to the large termite mound.

"The ants spent hundreds, thousands, probably million years to build the mound. It passed from generation to generation of ants. That's how the ecosystem works," said Mwila. Chisenga and I exchanged glances. We watched the ants going in and out of the reddish earth. "The birds make nests in the trees around the hill and feed on the ants, oblivious of the fact that without the ants, there would be no hill," she said emotionally. I wondered why she was going all philosophical on us. "Below this beautiful grass is copper. This savannah has hidden wealth," said Mwila as she led the way back to the path. We got on the Eagle and rode away.

Chapter 10

Eventually, the footpath joined the main road. Often, a fleet of light grey vehicles sped on the gravel road. We saw heavy lorries laden with farm produce struggling to climb the hills where the paths cut through. Traffic appeared on the mountains and disappeared down the valleys. I wondered where exactly the turn was.

We had been riding now for over three hours, but it seemed the journey was never-ending. And somehow we seemed to be travelling along a long, long winding red earth gravel road that promised no destination. What lay at the end of this road? The dust far ahead of us told us the end was not yet.

Soon, however, we forgot our weariness, *filongoma* and woodlands. Tall trees surrounded either side of the road, blocking out much of the morning sun. My eyes were searching for this turn to the enormous gravel road. Finally, I saw it. I was astonished to see how wide the Shombe Malakata Road was. Its surrounding appeared rural.

"Over there!" said Mwila, "Behind our compound lies a chest of precious gems." I was astonished by the machinery, bulldozers, excavators, loaders, trucks, and diggers. It was like the equipment I saw when *Cogefar*, an Italian company, was constructing the Kitwe-Ndola dual carriageway. I jolted up when I heard Mwila exclaim, "Oh, so much equipment!" Chisenga hummed in agreement and pedalled hastily.

As we rode on the Shombe Malakata Road, we saw more and more stationary excavators, loaders and diggers on the side of the road hidden behind trees that waved along the way. Chisenga pedalled harder than before climbing a lot of kilometres of a hill.

I heard an engine. I did not know if it was behind or in front of us. The noise of the engine grew louder. As we climbed near the peak, the oncoming car came into view. Chisenga began to shake, and without much warning, the Eagle flew off the road.

"Owe! Owe!" cried Chisenga. We landed into a bush on the side of the road, Chisenga landing headfirst, and I toppled over him. A sharp pain travelled from my ankle up to the shin and rested in my hip. I tried to gather strength to move, but I could not. The bicycle wheels were spinning round and round.

"Chisenga!" I called out nervously. "Chisenga!"

He did not answer. I managed to pull my head up. A vast field of groundnuts, pumpkins and maize stretched from the side of the road to as far as my eyes could see. "This must be *ibala!* (cultivated land!)" I could not tell if I was in a trance or it was a real experience for me.

"Can you hear me?" A figure stood over me.

The voice was low and heavy. It was too low to be Mwila's and too heavy to be Chisenga's.

"Hello! I am here to help."

I could see much clearer as time progressed—it was a tall figure in a dark green outfit.

My imagination went wild. "PC Mambwe was following us," I thought, "He must have been tracking us all along." I reconciled myself to my fate, helplessly and in pain. "How long has he been standing here? How long has he been calling out?" I wondered.

"Do not move. A car hit your bicycle, and I am here to help you. Do you understand?" I became aware that his outfit was different from PC Mambwe's. It was camouflage and not the long-striped green. Then I noticed a red cap on his head, a big decorous medal like a watch, assuring me that he was not PC Mambwe.

"Can you hear me?" he asked again.

I nodded.

He scooped me off Chisenga and laid me on the ground near the groundnuts mound. It was a vast field of groundnuts. On the edge of the area were maize plants with beans vines climbing on them. The stalks of maize were no taller than one metre, and the pumpkins and bean vines competed for the maize stalks.

A realisation dawned when I saw a second officer carrying Mwila. The impact of the car was significant. Mwila had been thrown in a ditch some metres away from us. She was covered in mud.

"Are you okay?" The second officer asked Mwila.

"I am terrified," said Mwila.

"Breathe!" The first officer said to Chisenga, "Keep breathing!"

Slowly, Chisenga lifted himself off the ground, staggered and was about to fall when the first officer caught him.

Helping him, the officer said, "Stay down."

"A Peugeot 404 hit your bicycle," said the first officer. As I listened to the army officer, my heartbeat was racing, and the headache was getting worse. The cars continued speeding on the Shombe Malakata Road.

"What's your name?" The first officer asked.

"Mwila Muma!"

"And you?"

"Lumba Chuma."

"Chisenga Waluse."

"I am Major Zulu, and this is Captain Phiri." The Good Samaritan officers were from the Zambian Army.

"Where are you going?"

"To the *mabala*," Mwila lied.

"Where do you feel pain?" asked the Major.

"In my hip and I have a headache," I said.

"In my ribs," said Chisenga.

"Everywhere," said Mwila.

The examination was quick. It appeared to me the officers were more interested in our breathing than broken bones.

"It's more important that you are alive. Except for a few bruises, I do not think you have damaged anything," said the Major calmly.

"Come with me. I can dress your bruises." We rose slowly and walked through the fields to the checkpoint where they camped.

We climbed into the army vehicle and sat on the benches. Major Zulu examined Mwila a bit more thorough than before, scrubbing the cuts. He took out plasters, mutton cloths, and *Dettol* from his first-aid box. He turned to me. "Lumba?" I was pleased that he could remember my name.

"Yes, Major" I responded. The examination was quick. Then, he turned to Chisenga and did the same.

"Where did you say you are going?" asked the Major.

"To weed out the *mabala*," Mwila repeated the lie.

"Where is the field?" asked the Major.

"A kilometre from here," she lied with a straight face.

I wondered as to how long she would keep lying. Chisenga avoided eye contact.

"Where is your hoe?"

"A hoe?" she said with a fake surprise. The Major turned and looked at Chisenga and me. All this time, Captain Phiri kept silent, studying our faces.

"Yes, the one you use for weeding?" said the Major. His tone was a bit sharp.

"We leave the tools in the field." She lied again. An uneasy feeling began in my stomach. I wanted to scream, "You are lying!" Then I calmed myself and wondered whether Mwila was a born liar or she was in a temporal survival mode. It was not that I could make the distinction between the two, or one or the other was excusable or tolerable.

"A container of water? Something to drink. Munkoyo, Mazoe or Thobwa?" pressed the Major. Mwila did not have an answer. On a thought of what to drink, I became thirsty. I wondered where the bottle of water we had tied to the bicycle was. Did it fall in *filongoma*? Did the impact throw it alongside Mwila?

"And your clothes? Will you change them at the field as well?" the Major said, shaking his head, and I sensed he could tell Mwila was lying. The army officers looked at each other nonplussed.

"No, Major. We came to see the new mine." Mwila began to tell the truth.

"To do what?" asked Major Zulu in surprise, his voice rising. And I wanted to know the reason too. It's the same question I had asked. And all I got was, "Trust me, Lumba."

Now she could not offer a spontaneous response. We sat in silence for what seemed a long time. None of us had any words to the officers.

Major Zulu stared at us.

"The Daily Newspaper reported a new emerald mine," said Mwila.

There was silence. Major Zulu and Captain Phiri exchanged glances. Chisenga looked at me.

"It's dangerous out here. The further you go towards the emeralds fields, the more dangerous it becomes."

The Major paused. A heavy sigh came from Mwila. I did not know what to expect when he looked at me.

"Where do you live, Lumba?"

"We all live in Chamboli Mine Compound," I said.

"Now we need to take you back to the compound." We were driven back to the mine compound in an army Magirus vehicle.

Chapter 11

J was glad not to find anyone at home because it would have been difficult to explain where I had disappeared. What explanation would I give?

"Well, a girl I fancy has some issues to sort out with Mukuba Mining Corporation. I know you do not know her. Not that I know her any better. She dragged me to the emerald mining field, and I have a headache and a pain on my left knee."

It was a relief not to have to say anything because I was such a poor liar, and the truth would have made me look so foolish. I lay on the sofa, shoes on my feet, trying to get rid of the sleepless nights' fatigue.

Tear gas canisters and deep excavations and Peugeot 404s flashed in my mind. I squeezed my eyes shut and prayed the scary thoughts would cease.

"I need to sleep," but failed to get into that deep, restful sleep that I needed so badly. I tossed and turned. The music from Nkote Club blustered, as my head pounded. The room was spinning, and canisters were exploding, the bicycle was shaking between the narrow slip of the deep excavations. I was fatigued. "I have a headache," I said to myself.

Putting on a clean shirt, shorts, and sleepers, I staggered out of the cabin in search of painkillers. "Where can I find *Caffeno*?" I thought. The shops were busy. Christmas music played from Fyonse General Dealers and the Asian Shopping Store. Walking gingerly, I saw women carrying baskets full of merchandise. Some were not in a hurry. I could hear gossip about PC Mambwe. "A paramilitary officer is roaming about," said one woman.

"He's looking for looters," another woman said.

"Who started the riots?"

"Why did they start it?"

Listening to the women, I wondered what intelligence PC Mambwe had gathered from all this chatter. I searched the corridor as I was worried the women had spotted PC Mambwe somewhere in the vicinity. Satisfied PC Mambwe was not there, I proceeded to the stores, bought some *Caffenos*, went back home and slept.

Chapter 12

When I got up from the deep sleep, the pain had gone. I do not know whether it was due to the painkillers or the deep sleep, but it was wonderful to feel so good. I stood outside in the summer sun that was warm but had lost its sharp midday sting. It hung on a cloudless sky like a big yellow round ball behind the mineshaft. The wind blew and brought with it the sound of the ventilation fans from the M Section.

Except for the fans, it was quiet. The five PM alarm had not wailed. It was not yet time when the compound came alive with children going home from school, music thumping from the taverns and clubs, and evening markets settling under the streetlights. The Kalukungu Road was empty for now, but in a few hours, it would be swarming with boys and girls crossing from the P to the L Sections and vice versa. I crossed the road and turned right, passing under the mutuntulwa trees not sure where to go.

I looked over to the Housing Office, and I saw a queue. I guessed it was township people reporting faults. A house in the compound had a leaking pipe, a broken window, or a door handle that was not working correctly.

A woman was knitting a scarf, a skill I saw among women in the mine compound. She was coming out of the Housing Office carrying electric bulbs. I thought about Mwila. I did not believe Mwila had such a talent. "How can a young woman who is so calculating have such skills?" I thought. The woman disappeared, and I turned walking down to the Mogadishu Stadium, the main playground in the compound.

There was no tournament, but I could hear some sounds coming from there. It looked like football training was going on. Walking along the terrace, I spotted the children's playground and went down to watch. Young girls were engrossed in the game of netball, and young boys were playing football. Another team of boys and girls played volleyball. They did not notice me, not that they needed to know that I was watching them. The games did not appear competitive either, so I carried on watching without concentration.

I came to the changing room and noticed the lights were on and stopped to look inside. Boys and girls played table tennis without trainers or white shorts. It was strange. During the days of prosperity, when all shops got their orders, games had a standard of dressing, and this one fell far short. "Lumba, who do you trust?" Mwila's voice echoed in my mind. It hit me Mukuba Mining would be selling the stadium if Micky was right.

I began to feel hollow. I tried so hard to enjoy the game and making something out of the trip to the stadium. I did not have to come here. It was the voice of Mwila that brought me out. "Mukuba Mining Corporation will sell the stadium." Her voice was sharp even when she was not there.

Every time the ball bounced off, either on the table or the walls, I felt the pain. It was not the physical pain which had been conquered by *Caffeno* and some sleep. Instead, it was an affliction of my soul. I felt sorry for the boys and girls, for myself and all the township people. I felt sad for the future of my compound.

And so, I looked away. If I turned left, I would be walking back into the miseries, to watch the games that would be no more. I did not want to prolong the pain. Instead, I turned right, walked briskly towards the Housing Office, and turned into the Kalukungu Road. A bird sang from the tree. Wearily, I dragged on.

I heard the alarm from the underground mine. A glance at my watch confirmed it was now five PM. It was evening. The time when the compound came to life, and I loved it. But the joy of the township had left me.

A group of boys and girls were yelling at each other, knocking off Ucar, BEREC, Spark, and Tiger batteries. It was a game I played when I was young. I did not stop to watch it.

I turned a corner. Under the light of the streetlamp, a column of boys and girls filled up. Someone shouted a letter. The queue moved to the new alphabet. One did not move, and another went against the majority. I walked away from it, dragging my feet on the road. But the singing of the bird was still there on my mind. It was dear, keeping me company.

A ring of older boys and girls attracted spectators. It was intense drumming, singing, clapping, and dancing. Chamboli was pulsating everywhere except in my heart. I felt I was the only one that cared about the compound.

Walking along Kalukungu Road, I heard miners from the underground mine talking about *Chibuku*. "The beer at Mwabonwa is always the best," they said. *"Tamwaba fikapa.* (There are no corn husks to throw away.) "They laughed. I followed them towards the sound of music. The men spoke in loud voices; the easy banter between them showed their camaraderie. But I enjoyed none of it.

Walking behind miners, I passed young men shuffling on a bridge for best spots. Then I noticed a crowd scrambling for areas to watch from. I stopped and scanned the milling crowd. Across the road was the Mwabonwa Tavern and people were streaming in. At the gate was a busy queue. The seating spaces inside and outside the tavern were full of patrons revelling to the tune of the Serenje Kalindula band. It was live music.

The bylaws on the side of the gate revealed the beer hall opened at three o'clock in the afternoon and would close at midnight. They admitted only adults over eighteen years old. I waited to enter.

"Your age?" the bouncer asked.

"Nineteen," I said.

He did not take long to size me up. "You are not coming in." And that was the end of the story. I could not enter the establishment. Frustrated, I looked inside the tavern from the wire fence. I watched the miners laughing. They took out their wallets and counted the money—a container of *Chibuku* on their table.

I walked away from Mwabonwa feeling lost and lonely. I did not need to enter the beer hall. I desperately wanted to silence Mwila's voice with loud music. "Lumba, there's no turning back," her voice echoed. "If the paramilitary officers enter the parish, put your hands as if in prayer." I stood still, but her voice still echoed in my mind. "How will I clear my head now?" I asked myself.

I walked along a narrow pathway and emerged at Nkote Club. Here the Masasu Band played the music, and the Club's veranda was a stage for their drum sets, big speakers, band members and dancing women. I saw an attendant move about with bottles of Mosi Lager serving their patrons. I felt lonely and hung my hands on the fence and stared at the front porch blankly. I wanted to talk to somebody. But what would I talk about?

"Lumba!" I turned. It was Mr Phiri wearing a worried look. "Chisenga has just passed here, looking unwell, and was dragging himself to the J Clinic." My hands dropped off the wire fence and flopped on to my side. "When?"

"Just now." Mr Phiri turned in the direction of J Clinic. I followed his gaze and did not see Chisenga.

Chapter 13

*H*urriedly, I left Nkote Club searching in the dim street. The moon was becoming bright, but the stars could hardly be seen. It was quiet on the mutuntulwa tree-lined road.

I saw no one until I reached the J Clinic, a single floor complex surrounded by a well-maintained garden of roses, lilies, and hibiscus flowers. Sidewalks were kept neat and tidy. I passed three ambulances in the emergency parking lot. Then, the signposts guided me to the reception area, and I began to search for Chisenga there.

The reception was having a busy evening. Chisenga was at the front of the queue. Behind the reception desk were shelves of medical cards that covered all the four walls from the floor to the ceiling. I took my place by the side of Chisenga just as the receptionist asked, "Mine number?"

I consulted Chisenga. "19770810", I said. The receptionist did not have trouble to retrieve the card. I placed the white medical card under my armpit and supported a staggering Chisenga. His groans disturbed the quietness in the waiting area, which was full of faces of patients that were suppressing the signs of pain. They had wrapped arms around their chests.

As if to follow suit, Chisenga put his hand on his chest, labouring to breathe. We waited ten minutes before the door opened again. When the medical officer emerged, she shouted a name. A patient rose and followed the medical staff. My gaze followed the medical staff as she walked ahead of the patient until they disappeared at the end of the long hall, labelled "Radiology."

A man carried a woman towards the radiology. And then a medic appeared and helped him. The woman seemed in pain, coughing hard, pulling along a cylinder-like machine. Nurses wheeled an empty bed in the passage, and put the woman on it, while they gave her medicines. Her lung-tearing cough ended. Quickly, the medics wheeled her away while she held desperately to the tube from the cylinder. All the while, I sat quietly and watched nervously.

A few minutes later, another medic appeared and called out a name. Not Chisenga. However, Chisenga rose and staggered towards the radiology department. Following behind him, I held on to his medical card and steadied him along the way. He opened the door. I was hoping to see a bed or anything that Chisenga could collapse on. However, there was no bed in sight. I noticed two chairs, a table, a bench, and a watercooler. There were no patients, no member of staff. I wondered where those answering to their names were disappearing to.

A sign identified the room as "Waiting Room/Nurses' Station." Chisenga turned around to face the bench and dropped himself on to it. I watched him lay flat on his back, and he groaned. "Are you okay?" I asked, and he gave me a groan. "No, Lumba." That was all the answer I got from him. Holding his ribs in pain, he pointed to the door. I obliged, walked off and searched for help. The corridors in the radiology were long and winding. The walls were painted white, and the smell was the typical hospital smell of *Dettol* or *Savlon*.

I froze on my feet when the Doctor came towards me. Her kind face immediately relieved some of the anxiety that had built up in me. "My name is Doctor Beenzu. I am the head of the radiology department. Can I help you?" asked a beautiful woman in a white coat with a stethoscope around her neck.

"My friend ... my friend collapsed." I stammered. Doctor Beenzu wore a searching look. I turned around, and she followed me to the nurses' station. Kneeling near the bench, she placed the back of her palm on Chisenga's neck. Chisenga did not move. She parted his eyes and seeing the Doctor, Chisenga crossed his arms on his chest and groaned heavily.

"A car hit him. It hit both of us." I realised I was not making much sense to her. Doctor Beenzu gave me an "I don't understand you" look and moved her gaze to Chisenga, who now, had coiled himself up, and began to cough. The Doctor called for a nurse, and together they put Chisenga on a wheelchair. They wheeled him into a quiet examination room.

"Name?" she asked.

"Chisenga," I said on his behalf. Chisenga groaned. I passed the medical card to Doctor Beenzu, who skimmed the old notes and flipped the card.

"Age?"

"Nineteen."

She scribbled the details.

I was startled by the flickering lights and the buzzing machines. Laying the card down, Doctor Beenzu gestured to me, and we hoisted Chisenga from the wheelchair on to a bed. Doctor Beenzu pulled Chisenga's shirt up, moving the stethoscope on his chest, here and there.

"Breathe in. Breathe out," Doctor Beenzu said coolly.

Chisenga looked scared. I was nervous too surrounded by strange sounds, flashing lights and sharp instruments on the trolley. Doctor Beenzu picked up one of the terrifying tools attached to the device and stuck the thin spiked end in Chisenga's ribs. He did not flinch.

"Do you feel a sharp prick in your ribs?" asked Doctor Beenzu in a flat tone.

"Why?" asked Chisenga lying face down. His response surprised me.

"I am examining heavy metal contamination," said Doctor Beenzu, which worried me even more.

"Am I poisoned?" Chisenga cried.

"Do not panic. It is a standard screening process to establish exposure."

"Exposure to what?" I asked.

"We have noticed cases of high metal contamination due to breathing in air from the copper smelters." Doctor Beenzu examined Chisenga's neck and armpits.

"What does exposure to…?" I said nervously missing the metal contamination.

"The contamination lowers immunity and reduces the number of lymphocytes, the cells responsible for antibody production," she said.

Unsticking the scary tool from Chisenga's back, she wrapped the blood pressure machine on his arm and took the reading. Then, she popped a thermometer into Chisenga's armpit and began to ask question after question.

"Do you get headaches frequently?"

"Do you feel weak?"

"Have you ever collapsed without cause?"

"Are you a miner?"

"Have you visited the smelter recently?"

Answering, "no", to all the questions, Chisenga began to sweat. It was clear he was in pain. I feared the scary machine confirmed Chisenga was contaminated. Doctor Beenzu moved away from the bed to the trolley of tools. She arranged the tools and fixed some to the scary machine, leaving my mind wandering from Chisenga to her.

"Cough?" she said calmly.

Chisenga coughed. She laid a towel on his frightened face.

"Cough?" she said again. Chisenga coughed warily.

I saw a red tube — one of the three attached to Chisenga. The fluid flowed from Chisenga into the machine. I suspected the device was drawing blood from Chisenga. Moving towards the door, I began to feel sick.

When she turned on a button, the scary machine ejected a plate that hung over Chisenga's chest. "I will take an X-ray," she said. Walking towards the door, I followed her, and we stood in the quiet corridor illuminated by signs and notices. Doctor Beenzu closed the entrance to the examination room. "You can now wait for your friend from the nurses' station." She had a look that one could not read on her face.

The journey to the nurses' station felt long and tiring. I dragged my feet, looking over my shoulders. Doctor Beenzu was still standing on the corridor, pressing buttons. Lights flashed red; ringers sounded beeps. I could not tell if the flashes and beeps came from the examination room or the hallways.

I opened the door to the nurses' station and let my weight drop slowly on to a bench. I wondered about Chisenga's pains. "Was he suffering from the impact of the bicycle accident? Or did the dust on Shombe Malakata Road clog his lungs?" I thought. I gazed around the room, counting the furniture, which helped to calm my nerves.

I shifted my gaze from the furniture to the walls and saw pictures of broken skulls, arms, ribs, shoulders, and legs. I could not stay still and moved closer to the images. The date scribbled on the pictures was the first of December 1986. I began to think of the township people. I did not know anyone who had broken a bone recently. I heard no whispers from the shop corridors of the injured escaping teargas canister or PC Mambwe. Then I remembered the men described by Micky. "Are these bones of the friends of the market vendors?" I thought.

"Lumba?" I sat up straight and stared at Doctor Beenzu, a folder on a table in front of her. I might have dozed off, and the door must have been open. Doctor Beenzu was sitting next to Chisenga. I wondered if the scary machine confirmed the contamination. I waited to hear if the plate detected any broken bones.

"The X-ray shows no broken ribs," she announced. Chisenga sighed with relief, and I nodded. Doctor Beenzu acknowledged me and consulted the notes. Raising her head, she said, "The blood test showed sulphur dioxide particles." The news came as a complete shock.

I looked at Chisenga, and I thought, "Am I also contaminated? How did this happen to my friend?" I let out a long sigh and realise I had been holding my breath.

"Sulphur dioxide agents are causing asthmatic symptoms. The results are not conclusive to show that you have developed any disease or tissue damage. I have not completed the full examination, so I will be sending a sample to Wusakile Mine Hospital for further tests to come in by next week. Now, Chisenga will not go home. I will keep him for observation in Mukula Ward."

I had stopped listening. I was wondering why I did not react. I was afraid to ask questions. What if Doctor Beenzu conducted the tests, and I found that I too, although without pain, my heart was pumping poisonous blood around my body. I realised the thoughts had accelerated my heartbeats. I wanted to reach out and wrap my arms around Chisenga, but that would be awkward. We only did that when we played football in the under-fourteen tournaments. We hugged when we were delighted with a win but not when sad and confused.

I pushed myself further back on the bench. Doctor Beenzu passed a packet of medicines she had prescribed for Chisenga, who seemed to be in deep thought. "But where did sulphur dioxide come from?" Chisenga had finally found his voice. It was a question that I was also thinking about.

"The *Senta* this morning was stronger than usual, and the average SO2 levels reached asthmatic irritation levels. My department has been receiving patients for the whole day." Chisenga and I looked at each other. I could see fear in his eyes, and I wondered whether I have managed to hide mine for his sake.

"Patients living with lung conditions have been affected the most. Exposure to sulphur dioxide at a high level of concentration in 24 hours can cause premature death," Doctor Beenzu paused. My heart rate sped up. "Today, I treated a lot of residents with existing respiratory ailments such as asthma and tuberculosis," she was pointing in the direction behind her chair. "The beds on the Mukula Ward have been filled up by my patients," she said. A long pause followed, filled in by the humming sounds of machines.

The memory of a strong twiggy, dry, and rotten egg smell hit my nostrils. It was no longer PC Mambwe I had to worry about, but the Mukuba Mining Corporation and the *Senta*. I saw Doctor Beenzu put the folder aside. There was no more to be said. Chisenga turned towards me and met my gaze. He was rising from the chair when Doctor Beenzu asked, "Oh, tell me about the bicycle accident again? How did it happen? Did you cycle into a busy road?" she asked, flapping her eyes with wonder.

"I did not know the Shombe Malakata Road could be so busy in the morning. There were a lot of speeding vehicles. I just saw a Peugeot 404 emerge through the dust, and the next minute, we were all sprawled in a groundnut field," said Chisenga.

If Doctor Beenzu was sceptical about the story, she did not show it. Her face was straight and attentive. "My machines did not show broken bones on you," she said and smiled. There was a brief silence. I looked at the images of broken bones on the wall.

Doctor Beenzu stared at me. She was trying to read my mind, but she did not turn to look at the pictures. I kept looking at the images of broken bones. Slowly, I shifted my gaze. On the adjacent wall, were pictures of lungs. I stood up and went close to the images. I did not see any dates on them. "What are the circles and crosses for?" I asked.

"Severity of the damage." She said. "I label my lungs." I wondered why she personalised lungs on a picture. I turned around to face her. Standing up, she placed her fingers on the images. "If the damage is severe, I circle the affected area." She traced on some of the circles on lungs, airways, and windpipes. Walking further along the wall, she pointed at crosses, "When the impact of the contaminant is not serious, I mark them with crosses." I saw a pen hanging on the pocket of Doctor Beenzu, and I wondered what label Chisenga's lungs would receive.

"What is going on in the township?" I sighed, walking home alone. I left Chisenga in the J Clinic. On that day, I realised there was much that the township people could not control. Waking up early in the morning and riding bicycles around deep pits was in our control. Anyone could decide to stay home or risk one's life in the dark. However, waking up early in the morning and breathing lousy air was not avoidable. It only led to the examination of the lungs under scary machines—the images which haunted me all the way home. And the voice of Mwila that tormented my mind vanished as this reality sank in.

Chapter 14

One of the things that amazed me in the compound was how tailors and shoe repairers could talk to their customers while they were busy with the work on hand. Mwila and I sat on stools, listening to the conversations while catching the morning sun. Several tailors lined up the shops, and the Chamboli residents waited. Others babbled happily, creating a melody in my ear as they drifted past the corridors roaming in and out of the stores.

Mr Phiri's radio tuned to the Zambia Broadcasting Services, and the news was about the looting in the township. No one paid attention to the information on the radio. So, I turned to Mwila, but she had her ears to the conversations on the corridors. I attempted in vain to distract her while I was tensing up, constructing scenarios for the day ahead.

Eventually, the last customer for Mr Phiri's services left. And Mwila's questions came instantaneously. I guessed it right. It was about minerals and Mukuba Mining Corporation. "I do not know how far I should go with this." Mr Phiri paused his response while he tightened a cotton thread on his sewing machine.

"In the 1800s economic depression hit Europe. The loss of wealth led the British to seek cheap sources of raw materials to revamp and grow their industries. They strolled around here exploiting every mineral wealth they could lay their hands on. Emeralds, copper, magnesium, cobalt, and many more were shipped to Europe." I wondered how a simple tailor was so well informed. I was suspicious of Mwila's interest in such stories. However, I was beginning to be curious about the history of the compound as well.

"How did they go about exploiting the minerals?" asked Mwila.

"They hired John Cecil Rhodes. He was a ruthless businessman. He secured most of the Southern African region," Mr Phiri said. And I wondered if Mr Phiri wanted to show us John Cecil Rhodes caused the looting of the past week. I could not see how events that happened hundreds of years ago would have an impact on us.

"That's a vast region," I said.

"Yes from the Limpopo to our mighty Zambezi River and up to the Luapula River, hiring mining companies to excavate the grounds. He wanted the whole African from Cape to Cairo."

"Did John Cecil Rhodes just show up and took the mines?" I asked knowing too well that was not how I would expect things to have happened.

"It was not like that. Rhodes was known to the colonial office in London. When he arrived, he signed treaties with our local chiefs to allow him access to minerals and claimed our land for himself." Mr Phiri paused again. I could tell the riots had created a backlog for him. I wondered why he accepted to mend more clothes when he had twenty-four hours in a day like everyone else.

The pause ended up being twenty minutes. Mwila and I turned towards the mineshaft across the river. The sun had risen over the two big wheels. They were not spinning, for it was not time to bring up the miners from the underground mine.

Pointing to the mineshaft, Mr Phiri said, "Rhodes' BSA company sunk the shaft, hired the Anglo-American Company, who built the township. Ever since they have been collecting large sums of money from the minerals of our land."

My eyes fell on the birds when my brain wandered off again, continually searching for the conversations for a trip ahead. It was a swarm of black *tumimbya* birds. They flew up and up, covering almost an entire township sky, obscuring the view of the mineshaft. I shifted my gaze to Mwila. She did not see the spectacle and did not notice me. All she did was asking questions.

"How many stones have they taken away from here?" asked Mwila.

"Millions and millions of tonnes from this region. The country was a third world producer of copper after the United States and the Soviet Union," said Mr Phiri, causing Mwila to twitch.

"Mukuba Mining Corporation complains that they are making losses, but they want to buy the emerald mine," said Mwila shaking her head, fidgeting on the stool. She was unaware that the sky had opened up again. The *tumimbya* birds were now flying over Wusakile mine township or Ndeke compound. There was no way I would have known.

All the while, Mwila was moving her head away from the warm sun that peered through the mutuntulwa trees. Eventually, she turned her gaze inside the shop, and I followed suit. The clock on the wall showed ten minutes past ten. "Are you going somewhere?" asked Mr Phiri.

"Yes, I'm going to Kitwe Town Centre with Lumba!" Mwila looked in my direction, and I nodded.

"You should have said earlier. I was not going to waste your time with my stories. *Kalebalika mwebana*," he said, dismissing us with a blessing. With a thank you, we left him to his tailoring and headed for the bus station.

Arriving at ten-thirty at Chamboli bus station, Mwila and I stood under a tree waiting for a bus. There were two choices for us. We could go into the shelter for a coach service operated by the United Bus Company of Zambia, popularly known as UBZ, or remain under the tree for privately-owned minibuses.

The fact that we were very few at the bus station meant people had no money to travel around the Copperbelt. Moreover, it was neither the first nor the fifteen of the month. Anyone that lived in the township knew the station was busiest on two paydays. Wives of miners go to Kitwe Town Centre to top up supplies that shops in the compound can not provide. The miners did not have incentives to go outside the compound. The Masasu and Serenje Kalindula bands played live music from the Mwabonwa Tavern and Nkote Club that were never short of *Chibuku* and *Mosi Lager.*

"Would you like some Maheu?" Mwila asked, to which I said, "Yes, please." When Mwila stepped forward to make an order, the seller quickly dipped two plastic cups into the drum and drew smooth, sweet, and creamy Maheu.

We drank the Maheu slowly in the sunshine on the station bench while watching call boys directing the queue and selling newspapers.

The newspaper editors carried the same story for more than a week of the police appealing to anyone with information on the market vendors that started the riots. When a newspaper seller noticed my interest in the headline, he picked up a copy and handed it to me. I thanked him and began to peruse through the pages. I was not the only one reading without paying any money. A few township people lingered under the trees reading without taking the papers away. I supposed it was a perk for living in Chamboli to read newspapers for free. Most readers I saw had turned to the back page headlined, **Nkana Meets Power**, a football match scheduled for the coming weekend

A pile of magazines next to the newspapers caught my attention. Young readers of primary school age bought a copy and flipped the pages. They were soon engrossed in it. I heard them giggle. The faces of the youngsters gave it away why the back page of *Icengelo* was sweet and amusing by turns. "*Katona nomunankwe Ponyax, awe kwena balishupa* (Tona and his friend Ponyax are naughty again!)." I put down my newspaper to listen to their conversation.

"Do you think Tona lives at the parish?" asked one friend to the other. I waited for the answer, but it never came. It was the same question that baffled me when I was young. And I would later be disappointed to learn such maverick characters never lived at Chamboli parish. Instead, I would come to know that only Peter and Father Katyetye resided there. I began to wonder if Father Katyetye came up with some of the stories in this Catholic magazine, describing Peter or some other parishioner.

"Lumba!" Mwila startled me, shifting my gaze to her. "It would not matter much which bus service operator arrived first," she said. "All the buses are well maintained." She was oblivious of the Maheu, rolling on her pair of jeans.

I jumped up. "Careful!" I shouted, and instinctively leaned forward to wipe the drops. I stopped myself just in time and put my hands in my pocket.

Mwila smiled. From her brownish handbag, she retrieved some tissues and soaked the drink away. "Thanks." She said, smiling. My mind went off on a tangent. "Her purple lipstick just looked right on her," I thought.

I began to picture her with a stethoscope around her neck, holding a fountain pen ready to cross or circle on an image. Even when she put her cup on the shaky bench, it seemed to me as if it was some mixture to make us survive the *Senta*. I worried every day that went by we breathed toxic gases from the mines. Mwila would one day join Doctor Beenzu to measure the toxicity of the gases from the copper mines.

When I could finally focus, I thought I was seeing it for the first time. On one of her fingers that grasped the cup of Maheu, I noticed that Mwila wore a ring. When it glittered, I felt numb like my heart stopped pounding for a minute or two. I looked down and waited for the agonising moments to pass, took a sip from my cup and lifted my gaze.

Just in time, a Toyota Rosa minibus arrived. It wound its way through the narrow first street in *ma New* section and stopped at the station. The bus opened its doors, and a dozen passengers disembarked. Mwila and I found

seats next to each other on the bus that was playing Bob
Marley's music from a radio. The temperature inside was
a few degrees higher than outside. Hooting as the engine
roared, the driver pulled the minibus out of the bus station
gathering speed when it joined the Kalukungu Road. The
call boys faded away, and the mutuntulwa trees on the busy
avenue came in sight.

I rested my gaze on Mwila, who was busy watching the
trees fly past. My mind wandered again. Mwila reminded
me so much of Doctor Beenzu. They seemed to have a
certain amount of similarities I could not put my finger on.
I turned my gaze from her and preoccupied myself with the
beautiful views that came and went.

I heard joyful noises from outside the bus. The township
children threw mutuntulwa fruits at the birds, and the
migrant *tumimbya* birds flew higher than the mutuntulwa
fruits could reach. When the fruits began to descend, the
birds clamped the wings and went into a gravitational free-
fall. Before the birds could hit the ground, they opened the
flaps and flew upwards. And then the children threw more
fruits at the birds. The lively children excitement went on
and on.

As the journey progressed, there were children flying
kites on an open field between the Mogadishu Stadium and
the J Clinic, while others were chasing grasshoppers. They
shouted, *"inshonkonono!"* and raced after the grasshoppers
that hid in the grass and thick mango trees. Climbing the
trees, the children shook the branches unsettling a variety
of green, brown and multi-colour striped grasshoppers.
They were quickly collected and put into empty bottles

of Tarino, Schweppes and TipTop. "Mwila, look!" I said, "They will sell them to vendors at Chamboli Market."

"Yes, Lumba, and they will end up at Nkote Club in the evening, fried and ready to eat," Mwila said with a smile.

"They are delicious," I said wistfully.

She parted the back of my hand as if to comfort me. "We can get some on our way back." I did not doubt her kindness of heart. After all, she had bought Maheu. So, I turned my hand, and I locked my fingers with hers. She did not protest.

The minibus took a corner. Immediately a greenfield opened ahead of us. A swarm of blackbirds with long tails performed a flying salute over the open fields giving me a consolatory feeling of a revitalised life, newness and hope for the township. I watched the birds ascending and circling over the ground. The birds had immigrated to the compound at the start of the rainy season in November. It was a familiar sight to me, although, every year, I was surprised at the first sighting of the birds. Township people were always excited about the arrival of the birds that came ahead of the rain season. The adults would predict the amount of rainfall by the timing and number of the birds that arrived. They talked about the birds that would stay in the township until the beginning of the cold season in May.

When the music stopped playing, my attention returned to what was happening inside the minibus. I looked at Mwila. Her hand still clasped in mine. She had a faraway look on her face. I wondered what had brought the expression of deep thought. "But she had just shown kindness to me. She had bought Maheu and offered a snack of *nshonkonono*," I thought. I pretended I was looking outside. I could see her eyes spoke of a beautiful soul. So, I felt I had done her wrong. But how could I undo it? I resented the feeling. Then I thought, "Perhaps that her personality. All I needed was to understand her." I knew it was a great idea and decided to say nothing in case she pulled her hand away from mine.

We crossed the Kamatemate Stream to Wusakile mine compound. The mineshaft came in close focus. The wheels on top of the shaft were turning, and the cables were rattling. Next to the shaft were the chimneys that released dark smoke in the air. We passed under the railway line bridge popularly known as the 16 feet opposite the Copperbelt Agriculture and Commercial Showgrounds. When we emerged, an imposing structure blocked the sun. Mwila pointed at the mine-dumps. "Lumba, can you see the high voltage electric train?" she said. The train was moving on the lofty cables on top of the slagheap.

"It's a *malamba*!" I said. The height of the copper waste deposit was remarkable. I thought it showed the length and breadth of the search for minerals. I took a tentative look at the train emptying the pots of molten mass from the underground, and I felt the temperature inside the minibus go up by many degrees.

"Lumba, did you know that the slag contains some valuable copper?" said Mwila.

I shook my head, pleased to see her light mood.

"My father told me the copper waste had over three per cent of good grade copper," she said. "We live in a compound that is rich in copper so much that a lot of it is wasted." I was not surprised at how much copper touched her feelings.

"Can you feel the heat, Mwila? This road will be a danger very soon," I said to spur her on.

"The mining company demolished houses and shops a few years ago. They moved residents around different sections of the compound," Mwila said, and I nodded not that I knew all the details.

"Lumba, the mining company can move graves and villages if they discover copper."

"How so?" I said.

Mwila's voice was calm, though a solemn expression settled on her face, "The Anglo-American Corporation moved the grave and the royal village here when it was a thicket locally called *Ukusakile*." I wondered whether the township got the name from the thickets.

"Where was the royal village originally?" I asked.

"On the other side of the mineshaft where the mining company has built the administration offices." I thought Mwila paused for effect. "If they discover any minerals, they can move us dead or alive," she added.

"Mukuba Mining cannot do that now, can they?" I asked.

"Many villages in Chief Nkana's area face eviction following Mr Buteko's decision to allocate their land to Mukuba Mining Corporation. The current chief Nkana does not know where to resettle his subjects facing eviction from the mining company." Unsure what to say, I kept quiet.

Gradually, the mineshaft receded behind us. A signpost showed we were no longer in Wusakile mine township. We had crossed to the other side of the mineshaft.

Chapter 15

With so many bus stops in Kitwe Town Centre, we got off on one near a rail station. The rumble of busses and trains and the noise of cars created a din that was unfamiliar to my ears. We strolled, hand in hand. Up the crowded streets and down the jammed roads, tall buildings nested Mwila and I. Expensive suits and watches in shop windows. I spotted outlets selling new and costly cars. Duly Motors. Central African Motors. Sundat Motors. Crown Motors. This side of Kitwe had more white cars than the yellow ones that moved around the mine compound.

When we crossed a full and busy road, a signpost that pointed in the direction of the University of Zambia at Ndola, UNZANDO, caught my attention.

"How did you get into university?" I asked Mwila.

"By sheer determination!"

I laughed.

"Why are you laughing?" she asked.

"I know, how determined you are," I responded, and she gave me a look.

"What course are you pursuing?"

"Bachelor's Degree in Accounting and Finance," she said.

"I thought you were studying Law," I said, and thereupon she elbowed me.

"Was this something that you always wanted to do?" I asked.

"Not really, Lumba. I wanted to go to the University of Zambia in Lusaka. Maybe read Law. I was not sure. Every student at Chamboli Secondary School seemed to know the courses at the Lusaka Campus and what they wanted to study. Not so with me. I did not have a clue. My father suggested the UNZANDO School of Business, Kitwe Campus and Mukuba Mining Corporation offered me a scholarship."

"That's amazing, Mwila. Do you like the course?" I asked.

"So far, so good."

"I found Principles of Accounts and Ordinary Level Mathematics interesting. I am hoping I will get good grades that would see me into a university. I cannot wait to leave my parent's home," I said.

"What course do you have in mind?"

"The same course as yours."

A pause. Mwila went quiet. Worryingly quiet.

"Mukuba Mining Corporation is no longer offering sponsorships. They discontinued in my second semester," she said. My eyebrows rose instinctively.

"Have they stopped offering bursaries for students already studying Accountancy?"

"Yes, Lumba, I do not know anyone from my course on the mine company bursary."

"How did you get through university without a bursary from the mine?"

Mwila sighed slowly and smiled at me, squeezing my hand gently. I felt reassured that she was interested in my questions.

"I was lucky I got a bursary from the government. It is not much though."

"So, how do you manage? Does your father pay some of your fees?"

"The inflationary pressures have eroded the value of the Kwacha. Mukuba Mining has not increased the salaries of the miners above rates of inflation for a long time. My father cannot afford to send me to university on his salary."

"Maybe, he would be promoted and earn a lot of money."

Mwila shook her head at my lack of understanding. "The problem with copper is that the price of the commodity is not set here in Zambia where it is mined. The market for copper is in London." Indeed, I did not understand much of what she was talking about. I began to imagine how one day I would appreciate it when my turn came to be at the university.

Suddenly, her hand movement became cautious and stiff. She focussed her gaze far off, through the thick green leaves of the mango trees. There stood out against the light blue sky, a red roof on a big house. The lawns were tidy, and the gardens were graciously big. It seemed to me this side of the mineshaft was very different from the area where I lived in Chamboli.

"Who lives in that house?" I asked. If I had not seen the plaque on the gate, I would have put it to her unpredictable responses. "The Chief Mine Captain of Mukuba Mining Corporation, of course. His yard can take twenty houses where we live!" moaned Mwila. I did not know if the Chief Mine Captain was more deserving of such a massive space. He was not the only one who lived in a mansion. We had earlier passed big houses and tidy gardens, manicured lawns. Unlike the homes in Chamboli mostly fenced in *lunsonga*, here the houses were in hedges of flowers, among which the hibiscuses, lilies and tulips flourished, and spilt out their colours.

"The mango trees are greener here than in the mining township," I said, still looking at this mansion. Mwila was quick to offer a reason. "When the mines designed the town, they built the mine compounds in the direction of the prevailing winds, making these compounds vulnerable to *Senta* emissions. The wind blows the toxic gases towards townships. We are the *Senta* downwind population, Lumba." I nodded, more for solidarity with her, wondering how she knew all this information. I looked around the property, endowed with beautiful trees and colourful leaves waving in the wind. I followed Mwila's gaze towards the sound of the lawnmower.

"What's the matter, Mwila?" I asked.

"He's there, Lumba!" she said tersely.

"I saw him before he turned on the lawnmower. He was watering the garden a minute ago," I said calmly.

"No! He drew the curtains. I saw him!" Mwila spoke with anger like someone betrayed, and the whole world needed to know she had finally located who had done it. She moved forward and then paused.

"The Chairman?" I asked.

She frowned and babbled, "Yes. It's him!" She seemed relieved. It was like something was holding her back. I observed her as she stood motionless.

We could have stood there forever, except for the lightning that flashed and the thunder that rambled near us. We ran in the empty street to beat the sky that was becoming dark. The wind blew gently at first but grew stronger and then got fierce. The mango trees dropped some of the fruit. The leaves and the branches fell off, making our way dark and scary.

The sun was sinking fast, and the darkness was approaching at the same rate. We concentrated our undivided attention on spotting one of the telephone booths so that we could take shelter before the rain poured down. We were halfway on the street when we got the first splatter of the shower. Immediately, we took refuge in the nearby telephone booth, hoping we could see out the storm. Strong winds and rain buffeted the telephone booth.

"The mine managers are kidding themselves. They cannot eat mangoes from this side of the mineshaft while the trees on the other side perish from *Senta*," said Mwila angrily. What she said was true, or at least I expected it to be true. I gave it a cowardly nod.

The rain drummed wildly. Fear and panic rose. And to distract ourselves, we started reading the emergency numbers. Number 1 for Nkana Mine Hospital. Number 2 for Wusakile Mine Hospital. Number 3 for the J Mine Clinic. Number 4 for the Mine Police Station. Number 5 for the Mine Fire Brigade. It was not enough to distract us from the sounds of the torrential downpour. It sounded like the ventilation fans from the M Section blowing copper particles and other wastes in forms of clouds of dust from the underground. With the winds growing louder and louder, for a moment, I thought we might need the Fire Brigade.

Then the rainfall eased off. Slowly, I stepped out of the shelter into the street. The strength of the wind had faded. I gestured to Mwila, and we resumed our journey. We walked briskly in the empty street. But I loved the smell of clean air after a torrential downpour of rain. I urged Mwila to hurry for I did not trust the storms on the Copperbelt.

Reaching the theatre, we waited on the queue for our turn to be admitted. More and more people jammed on the door. Eventually, the door swung open, the ticket controllers motioned for us to go in.

Pushing ourselves in the crowd, Mwila and I climbed the stairs and followed carpeted floors. One side of the corridor was decorated with some of the most celebrated personalities of the town of Kitwe. I recognised Lottie Mwale and The Witch Band. The next frames showed footballers from the Power Dynamos Football Club in Ndeke which included Peter Kaumba, Alex Chola, and Freddie Mwila. It was the stars from the Nkana Red Devils Football Club in Wusakile that caught my utmost attention. Joshua Longwe, John Kalusa, Kapambwe Mulenga. Then my thoughts were cut short by Mwila's question, "Lumba, what do you aspire for in life?".

"When I was young, I played in the under-fourteen football club for one reason only. I wanted to become like one of these stars. I wanted to be famous and win games for Nkana Red Devils," I said, pointing at Kapambwe Mulenga.

"Mukuba Mining has sold the stadium, and you will

never realise your dreams," said Mwila in a teasing tone. Although it has been long since I gave up the dream, at that moment, I had a flash of anger and regret, and a lump in my throat blocked the air passage forcing me to open my mouth and gulp some air.

I looked away. "What about going to university and becoming an accountant?" She asked me.

"That was not my dream when I was young. I never knew anything about it. If I could not be a miner, the only job I wanted was to play football. How about you?" Mwila did not respond with words. She pulled me to the pictures of the Masasu and the Serenje Kalindula Bands. "Did you want to be a musician?" I screamed.

"Yes," she said.

"But you only talked about Law and Accountancy," I said.

"It's a long story!" and she beckoned me to move on.

I opened the door on the second floor, and a magnificent room greeted us. The place was lit brightly with an entire interior covered in copper and emerald colours. We hustled among well-dressed men and women. A waiter relieved me of the umbrella, and I stood before her in a wet jumper. I felt sorry she got her beautiful attire splashed with rainwater. I entered the bright, carpeted, crowded hall, and caught sight of the mine captains and their wives holding hands. The majority of mine captains were in jackets, sat by themselves and did not pay attention to us. I felt out of place. Unlike the township people who welcome strangers, I felt the men that patronised the theatres were not friendly and had no idea of the hardships in the mine compound. I was afraid of their proximity. A waiter showed us seats in a corner.

"We did not reserve the seats," I said quickly.

"Here is the menu," said the waiter and left immediately. I followed her.

"We are not eating. We got mixed up on the way in. How can we get to the open gallery?" I said, patting my pockets.

"I do not have money for meals." She ignored my response and said, "The show has not started."

"Where is the open gallery, please?" I asked, worried the mine captains would realise that I did not belong and send us out unceremoniously. I regretted my idea of crossing from the township to come to this other side of the mineshaft where life was complicated. Instead, the waiter, with a smile, said, "Welcome to the hospitality business lounge. I cannot send you away, sir. I am following the rules," she insisted.

"I do not have money to pay for this food," I said again. Mwila, standing by my side, smiled and said, "We cannot afford this food."

"Dear sir and madam, the meals are free," said the waiter.

Relief of not going to pay for the meals brought me a smile. I was wondering why the waiter did not tell me earlier the meals were free of charge. I turned and noticed Mwila was still smiling. I thought now Mwila and I understood each other. We were becoming more like friends.

I pulled a chair for Mwila, and I sat next to her. Suddenly, I looked up for a moment—to smell the flowers, and at once became aware of the luxury that copper brought to the men and women that lived on the other side of the mineshaft. It was apparent to me that the Anglo-Americans set up the mineshaft in the middle, creating two separate experiences either side of the copper mine. I thought of the miners from Chamboli Mine Compound. "After a hard day's work underground, they go home to listen to the local bands and eat the everyday meal of *nshima* with *kapenta* (sardines). And here the mine captains feed on free meals offering a wide variety of food." I became envious of the mine captains and loathed the Mukuba Mining Corporation for perpetuating this disparity.

Then Mwila smiled at me. Her teeth were beautiful, and her face broke into dimples. And her eyes were bright. I wished we were just the two of us I would have kissed her. I smiled back at her. She stared at me then looked away. Shyly, I turned my gaze at the mine managers.

I began to recollect the mine captains' movements at the office where I went for my temporary job. The captains had simple tasks. They carried folders and papers that documented the destination of copper. I looked around the massive dinner hall and at the mine captains. "They eat free meals here when we have shortages of mealie-meal in the compound," I said and waited for Mwila to confirm. She leaned forward, patted my arm, and cupped her hands under her chin. She looked at me, thoughtfully. I exhaled in a silent snort. Then I became conscious of how quiet the hall was, except for the forks hitting the plates.

"Ready for the meals?" asked a waiter. She said it so quietly that I had to lean towards her to get what she was saying. "Are you ready to order?" she repeated.

We turned our attention to the menu, examining what was on offer.

"*Nshima*?" We both said at the same time. We looked at

each other, and Mwila smiled. I looked at her in amazement, feeling a rush of affection. It occurred to me that I had never seen a mysterious young woman like her before. How beautiful Mwila's face was when she smiled. It made her so amazingly charming, and the space around her seemed to grow brighter. I struggled to reconcile the beautiful smile she wore now, to the anger that consumed her occasionally. "It was more than occasionally," I thought. Mwila's looks captivated me. "I think she is in bondage," I judged her without knowing who she was. She looked at the menu, studied it for a while and looked up again. Our eyes met.

"Everything okay, Lumba?" she asked.

I dropped my gaze to the menu and pointed, "You said, *nshima.*"

"Selfish mine managers. They have all the meals you can think of. Imagine they have *nshima.*"

"Everyone loves *nshima.*"

"Yeah. The captains know how to keep the tables flowing," moaned Mwila, "But they cannot reverse food shortages that are ravaging the mine compounds."

"And they have stopped sponsoring education!" I added.

Mwila nodded.

She seemed pleased with my understanding. The waiter served us the meals. Shortly, Mwila had stopped eating. Before I could ask, she put the fork and knife down, washed her hands, and picked the *nshima* and *kapenta* with her fingers. I followed her ring finger for it was hard not to focus on the radiant ring. I moved my seat forward carefully. I did not want her to notice. "Is she engaged?" I wondered. I did not know what I was feeling, but one thing

I was sure of was that I wished it had been me that had slipped the ring onto her finger.

"Is everything okay?" I looked up and met her gaze, but the words had come from the waiter standing nearby with a quizzical look. "Why does she keep coming and going?" I wondered. I preferred to eat from the evening market at Nkote Club. There were no waiters to keep asking questions that were not necessary. The women that sold snacks never bothered their customers with "Is everything okay?" They had a better system in the townships," I said after the waiter had left.

"Yes, Lumba," said Mwila. "Whether it is a Maheu drink at the bus station or a *chikanda* (home made polony) at the evening market, sellers offer a taste sample to the customer.

"The *dyonko*!" I guessed what she was talking about.

"Yes, once the customer tastes *dyonko* and likes the food, which is almost always the case, then the customer buys."

"And one is left to eat in peace!" I added. Surprisingly, she laughed to a conversation that seemed not amusing to me. It was indescribable to watch her giggle. I joined in the laughter attracting the waiter to our table. I braced myself for another "Is everything okay?"

But the waiter said, "The show starts in five minutes." Chewing *kapenta*, Mwila hummed a silent approval.

"What's that, Mwila?" I asked.

"Lumba, the captains know how to cook *kapenta*."

"Yes, it tastes great just like in the compound," I said.

"That's why they come here. Can you see everyone is eating *kapenta*?" said Mwila.

"*Bonse tuli bantu!* (We are all human!)" I said.

"Everyone is a Zambian!" she said. "Smile, forgive and forget and be a little bit more Zambian!" Mwila laughed out loud at what she had said. We got up and wandered off in search of the venue.

I followed Mwila down two floors and entered a hallway. We found our seats. I was immediately surprised by the number of men and women dressed in expensive clothes all talking in English with accents I had never heard from the township. "Mine captains," I said under my breath, settling in the auditorium. At that moment, however, I was conscious of neither excitement nor displeasure. I extended my hand to Mwila, and she grabbed it. I drifted from the show and closed my eyes.

When the show was over, we hurried to the bus stop. It was nearly five PM, and the bus stop was crowded. The hustling commuters cut in front of us. It was hard to move.

"The bus to Chamboli has left," she said.

"There is a short cut we can take," I responded.

We took a passage through the beautiful mansions. Turning a corner, I saw the mine-dumps in the distance. The city houses were behind us now, and Wusakile lay on the other side. I shifted my eyes from the mine-dumps to Mwila.

"How was the performance?" I said.

"It was good. Didn't you see it?"

"No."

Mwila stopped and turned to me.

"Where were you?"

I did not answer, and she smiled.

The path was narrow, and I walked behind her. For the

first time, I saw her dark hair. It was beautiful. I wanted to touch it. And then I noticed her lovely legs. Her arms swung gracefully. When the way widened, I caught up with her immediately. We were step by step.

I could not resist her arm. She walked closer to me. We were silent, and I thought of something to say. "You are so beautiful." I wanted to whisper, but I could not marshall some courage. We passed the mine-dumps in silence.

And then we heard the noise. The clapping hands and yelling drew near. Mwila clung to my arm. She was taking little steps as we walked along a dust road in Wusakile township. Now and then she pulled me closer to herself.

I looked towards a hill. Up there was the Wusakile mine hospital. "Chisenga's blood samples were inside there. In some laboratory perhaps," I thought, staring at the massive brown brick structure. Anytime soon, Chisenga would know if he had some lung disease.

"What are you thinking?" Mwila said.

"Nothing," I said.

"Look!" she said, pointing.

A crowd of children formed a ring on the side of the street. And in the centre of the circle, two children hopped around and shouted at the top of their voices. The arms were flying. There was pushing and yelling.

We passed the children and saw a smaller group. A girl at the centre of a gathering was focussed. She threw a stone in the air. And swiftly, her hand was sweeping other stones inside a small circle. With a high degree of concentration, she caught the falling stone and threw it back in the air, pilling pebbles inside the ring. Everyone was quiet. "*Ichiyenga*," Mwila murmured. I moved close to see.

"Look here, Lumba."

I turned to see boys and girls running around.

"It's called '*Start.*'"

A girl put a bottle on a pile of sand. Her eyes darted around. She ducked the ball meant to hit her, knelt, and began to fill the bottle up with sand. There was a shout. She looked up, rose and jumped up, avoiding the ball. Her peers roared.

Then, the lamp posts flickered. "It is now seven PM, Lumba," she said. "We must cross the Kamatemate River before it is dark," Mwila added.

We passed small houses with small windows. Some houses were medium. Not bigger than where we lived. The streets grew wider, and there were a lot of people on them. The din of many voices was too great, and all we could hear was a hum.

Descending the hill, I seemed to hear a mighty roar. During the rain season, the little Kamatemate River rose wildly and was cruel to cross. Merciless waters were beating on the banks as painful memories surged of countless children of miners swept on a shaky bridge or on stones where a bridge should have been. I frowned at the mines' polluted river daring it to come near Mwila and me.

We crossed the angry Kamatemate River and passed through the silent dark Milemu forest, emerging to the streets where people flowed like it was day time. The stars were shining, and the moon was bright. Hand in hand, we made it back to Chamboli township.

Chapter 16

I opened my eyes and stared up at the ceiling. The light of day was in the room. Still, the morning was unusually cold as I made my way to the shops, excited to tell Mr Phiri about my adventures with Mwila. Instead, I found Chisenga on the quiet shop corridor, peeping through the glass windows.

"*Shani, boyi*! (Hello my friend)." I greeted Chisenga first.

"*Shani, boyi*!" he said.

"Where's Mr Phiri?" I asked.

"There's nobody here. No tailors, no shoe repairers, and no watch repairers."

"What do you have there?"

"A Disco watch. I brought it for a watch repairer to get it into working order," said Chisenga looking inside Fyonse General Dealers shop.

"The doors are closed," I said.

"I do not think they opened today," said Chisenga.

"Did you try *ba* Seki *pa* Siwila shop to repair your watch?" I asked.

"He was not there. Siwila Stores is closed. Masafwa Groceries is closed too."

"There are a lot of watch repairers *pa* Wusakile market *napa* F Section. Shall we go there?" I asked

"They are closed! Even *ba* F Chiko who repairs shoes seven days a week did not open his shop," said Chisenga shaking his head. There was silence.

"I do not think they opened today," said Chisenga.

"That machine seems to have seen better days," said Chisenga, pointing at Mr Phiri's Singer sewing machine in the middle of the shop.

"It is overused. Residents from Chamboli, Luangwa and Mulenga compounds are visiting the tailors more often now. It is not surprising in the wake of second-hand clothes," I said.

"What about second-hand clothes?" he asked, looking thoughtful.

"There was a long queue here yesterday for Mr Phiri. Many people brought clothes to adjust the waists and lengths."

"I know Salaula does not last."

"It is all because of the deepening problems at Mukuba Mining." I groaned disapprovingly.

"I have vowed never to wear any of them."

"I do not mind, "I said smoothing the corduroy that I had bought cheaply from Chamboli Market.

"That material looks expensive," said Chisenga.

"Yeah with a good wash and after pressing, it is tidy and trendy, "I said.

"Mr Phiri is like me," said Chisenga, "He does not trust second-hand clothes and vows never to wear any. He prefers clothes sewed by the Strand Tailors."

"That's a contradiction thinking of his tailoring business, "I said.

"By the way, the Strand Tailors and the clothing industries in Kitwe are closing down," I added.

"Are you serious about that, Lumba?" said Chisenga.

"I went to Kitwe Town with Mwila yesterday, and I saw a lot of shop windows all boarded up." It was a lie but did the trick. Chisenga stood in silence.

"We have been standing here for a long time. Now, I doubt Mr Phiri is coming," I said, pointing to the closed doors. I reached for the door handle and shook the ABUS locks. They were firmly secured.

"The shop will not open. Look at the notice." Chisenga ran his fingers against the glass door.

"Yes, you are right, boyi!" said Chisenga pointing at a notice on the inside of the shop. No Cooking Oil. No Mealie-Meal. No Sugar. No Bread.

"Halt! Halt!" I heard a sharp voice from the direction of the ZCBC Stores. The security guard from Zempya was shouting, his voice echoing in the corridor. He was running towards us. He blew his whistle, and his dog was charging. Realising we could not outrun the dog, Chisenga and I leaned our backs against the doors. Fierce eyes stared at us, and sharp claws came close to pulling my corduroy. I coiled.

"Looters! I got you, looters!" shouted the guard.

"We are not looters," Chisenga and I yelled in unison.

The security guard did not pay attention to our protests. He charged his dog at me. I pulled my leg away, hitting against the grill door in the process. A severe pain made me push my head back as I groaned, and as a result, I banged my head against the metal bars. The dog was ready to pounce on me. I was so terrified I felt my legs would fail to hold my weight. I was massaging my head while pleading to the guard not to set the dog on us. Just then, the dog jump towards Chisenga, and he pressed in on me, and we fell.

The guard kicked Chisenga in the ribs. I felt the pain in sympathy and wrapped my arms around my chest, a few inches from the sharp teeth of the dog. My hatred of the Zempya rose.

Through all this noise, I heard boots stomping across the veranda floor. The running feet got closer and closer. Suddenly, a towering figure of a man silhouetted on the shop window against the rising sun. I lifted my gaze to face him. PC Mambwe was panting, buttons almost bursting from the military uniform.

"I got them! They were planning to loot the shop," reported the guard in a loud voice. I did not like his tone and expression.

"No!" we cried.

"You look familiar," growled PC Mambwe, looking at Chisenga and then at me.

I glanced on the floor, avoiding eye contact with PC Mambwe.

"Look up, *mufana*! (young man)," yelled PC Mambwe, pacing the floor. I stared in the face of the paramilitary man, wondering what he would do next.

"We do not have a bicycle. What will PC Mambwe ask us this time?" I thought.

"What are you doing here?" PC Mambwe asked in a commanding voice. I was wondering what was so complicated that he had to question our presence. For all

I knew, the shops were not out of bounds. I looked at Chisenga. He shrugged his shoulders.

"We came to see Mr Phiri," I said, knowing too well Chisenga came for the watch repairer. "But what difference does that make," I thought.

"You are lying! I know that you are lying. Mr Phiri is not working today. Did he ask you to come here?" shouted PC Mambwe impatiently.

I waited for Chisenga to say something. He did not.

"You are looters!" yapped the paramilitary man.

"No!" we yelled back.

"Then what... are... you doing here!" PC Mambwe began to stammer, splashing saliva between words. He forced himself to stop. His voice reverberated in the corridors. When the echo ceased, our attention moved to Kalukungu Road. An IFA truck rumbled on the way carrying police officers in riot gears. PC Mambwe stared at the lorry. The vehicle disappeared, and there was silence.

My back was hurting as I leaned against the grill door. I looked at PC Mambwe, who turned to his junior. "What do we do?" said the paramilitary man. The guard shrugged his shoulders and drew a blank face. I thought the Zempya guard looked awkward in his dark blue uniform. He waited for instructions from PC Mambwe who was pulling the police baton from his belt. His eyes continuously wandered from here and there. When he focussed on me, my heart seemed to stop beating for a minute. He was running his hand across the teargas canisters.

"Do you know the men that pushed the wheelbarrow into the mealie-meal truck?" he asked.

"No!" I said, with a note of certainty in my voice.

"Where are the men that looted the Chimanga Changa lorry?" PC Mambwe's voice was rising.

"I do not know," I said, trying to sound calm while keeping my eyes on the baton.

"You must know. You live in the mine compound. Where are the market vendors?" PC Mambwe was fuming, and frustration showed on his face. He swung the baton around and raised it to shoulder height, ready to hit me. I was shaking. I looked to the left and then to the right. There was no way out. I closed my eyes, ready for what was to come. I was stiff, resigned to my fate. After a brief pause of terror, I slowly opened my eyes. The baton was pointing at me.

"I'm looking for market vendors and a young woman. They were hiding at the Catholic parish," yelled PC Mambwe, leaning forward. "The woman is about your age," PC Mambwe said. His frown was fierce.

"There are many young women of our age in the compound. We cannot help you, sir," said Chisenga.

"That's a bold answer, coming from someone on the floor," I thought.

"You are... You are lying." Droplets of saliva shot in all directions as he yelled. PC Mambwe was burning with anger. He shook the door in frustration setting off the alarm. Without warning, the dog jumped and raffled PC Mambwe's leg. We took the opportunity and dashed.

Chapter 17

It was early afternoon, and I could hear music playing from Nkote Club. It lightened my mood. As I sat in the cabin nursing my aches and pains, all I could do was to dream about Mwila. "You're coming tonight?" Mwila had asked. "Yes," I had promised her. I could hardly wait to see her again. But I worried about Mwila. The consolation was the paramilitary officer could not describe her.

I left home facing the direction of the mineshaft. Twilight was gathering fast, as I strolled through the gathering dusk, pushing in the crowd. My eyes widened to see the Kalukungu Road chocking with people. "Where were they this morning?" I was talking to myself.

The mineshaft alarm went off. Chamboli throbbed at five o'clock in the afternoon. A stream of children came on the street. Young people sang, and children played in the dust. Miners and residents moved up and down. The warmth and intense was everywhere.

Near the Mwabonwa tavern, the street was livelier. People stood laughing and talking while the music was tuning up. Strings strummed. Drumbeats reverberated. But I was losing patience with the siren, and I felt that it was ringing on and on. And everywhere, revellers walked about with containers of alcohol. The place reeked with the smell of Chibuku.

"Shall we have some Chibuku?" I heard one man say. He rose and joined a queue that wound along the wall of the tavern. A small window was open. Behind it came a bartender. He brought out white plastic containers which he put under a device that looked like a sandglass. When he turned on the pump, the opaque maize brown beer poured from glass bulbs. The bar attendant turned the globes five times, and the miner had in his hands five litres of Chibuku.

The conversation of the miners was all about football, "The under-fourteen champions league will be on this Saturday," they said. "How could they concern themselves with football when the shops were closing the doors?" I thought. I wondered if the miners knew the mine captains were serving free meals on the other side of the mineshaft.

"Sanctary City Football Club will win this year's tournament, and the cup will be coming home to the P Section. Little Chiefs will be humiliated." They all nodded and shook hands. I guessed they were all from the P Section. Between laughter and shaking hands, the men passed the five-litres container from one miner to the other. When they cleared the contents, another miner volunteered to pick up the bill. He stood up, the big cup in his hands, and queued up to the window.

I turned my attention to another group of miners leaving the Mwabonwa tavern. I followed them, listening to the life at the underground mine. Stopping at Nkote Club, we stood on the bridge overlooking the Club. A crowd lined up against the wire fence listening to Litande Ngoma played by the Masasu band.

More and more township people arrived. I was starting to get nervous as I was afraid of bumping into PC Mambwe. Anxiously, I searched the faces around me. I worried the paramilitary man might see me with Mwila, and he would whip me with his baton and kick me in the ribs and throw me to the Zempya's dog. Then I stopped worrying when I recalled PC Mambwe's trousers being roughed up by the dog. I took some satisfaction from it, and I left the bridge and found a spot on the wire fence.

I was so engrossed in the music that I did not see a friendly face approaching.

"Hello. Mr Phiri. You did not work today?" I said.

"The police have blocked the roads. They are inspecting traffic between Chamboli Mine Township and Mulenga compound," said Mr Phiri. He adjusted his hat and cleared his throat.

"Residents of Luangwa, Mulenga, Wusakile or Chamboli cannot socialise now." He retorted. I shook my head in sympathy. "I know. Things are getting worse, Mr Phiri. No mealie-meal, cooking oil, sugar and not even bread. There's a notice at the shop. I have never seen this before in our compound."

I turned my head towards women from the evening market, taking their wares to the spectators. *"Chikanda! Inswa! Nshonkonono!* Groundnuts!" they called out for customers. A vendor offered tasters to would-be customers. *"Dyonko!"* she said, picking up a small piece of *chikanda.* After tasting the *dyonko,* some bought the merchandise, but many of them left without parting away with their money.

I wondered how she was going to earn a living if all the goods ended in dyonko.

The music had stopped, and the band began to tune the instruments. "One two. One two. One two" echoed around. "*Lelo ni lelo!*" (Today is today). Everyone in the compound understood the meaning. It was a promise for a great evening ahead.

"Why have the police closed the roads?" I said as the beat of the music was starting to go up.

"They are worried about an uprising. Mukuba Mining Corporation is planning a reduction of the workforce," said Mr Phiri and handed me a copy of the Daily Newspaper. **Mukuba Mining Corporation To Send Workers Home** screamed the headlines. I paused for a moment and stared at the newspaper.

I looked in the direction of the mineshaft. The wheels were turning slowly at the underground mineshaft, and the black gases piped out from the smelter chimneys spiralled towards the mine compound. "We are the *Senta* downwind population, Lumba" echoed my mind. I was reorienting my mind for the location of Wusakile and Chamboli towships. "It was not accidental," I concluded. I was convinced now that the mining corporation was aware of it. They built townships in the path of *Senta* and the homes of mine captains away from the toxic gasses.

I tried to listen to Mr Phiri, but I was too distracted. The *Senta* occupied my mind. And then the music picked up and the noise increased as more people were arriving. But Mwila was not among them. Suddenly, a figure appeared that looked like PC Mambwe. I froze.

Chapter 18

Shadows were getting longer and darker as the evening sun was setting down. Initially, the air was clear, warm and fresh. Then the eyes began to itch, and people started coughing. "Mukuba Mining Corporation has released *Senta*," the township people said. The white fumes were heavy and thick and covered the entire compound. I began to worry about the scary machine in Doctor Beenzu's radiology department. "Chisenga's toxic levels must be rising. Doctor Beenzu's reception will be full tonight." I also worried about my toxic levels.

Women selling *inshonkonono*, *chikanda* and groundnuts circled the Club cold-calling pedestrians before they settled back for their evening market under the streetlights opposite the Club. I moved back to the wire fence gazing at the guitarist and the drummer. Dancers took to the stage. Wiggling their waists, the girls danced away on the front porch of the Nkote Club. Spectators went wild. Pushing and shoving for the best position to watch the dancing.

By seven PM, the sun had disappeared below the horizon and darkness fell on the mine compound. Chisenga emerged from among the spectators.

"I have been looking for you!" he said.

"I have been waiting for Mwila and you for a long time."

"The *Senta* is worrying me," he said, and I nodded.

We hadn't been standing long together when Chisenga prodded me in the ribs and said, "Mwila!"

"Where?" I asked.

"Look at the bridge!" he yelled.

Mwila was crossing over the bridge, coming slowly towards Chisenga and me. "She must have seen us." I thought. Her skirt was above the knee, and the top was extended slightly below the waist, sleeves rolled to the elbow, showing her brown arms. In her canvas shoes, Mwila looked beautiful.

I thought she was going to shake hands with me. Then she opened her arms. The bear hug was warm.

"What for?" I asked while she held me tight.

"Just," she said and continued to hold me. Chisenga waited for his turn. Slowly she released the embrace and shook hands with Chisenga.

"PC Mambwe has been asking questions. He is looking for market vendors." Chisenga paused and looked at me. I shrugged my shoulders

"That's nothing new to me," Mwila said, looking at me.

"Something else." Said Chisenga, clearing his throat.

"What?" gasped Mwila. "PC Mambwe is looking for you." Chisenga let the words hung in the air, but Mwila did not seem moved.

"He is vague with the descriptions: Nothing close to identifying you. He does not have a photograph, and he has a bad memory." I said to reassure Mwila, but she showed no emotions. Shrugging her shoulders, she pulled me into the crowd, away from Chisenga who showed a quizzical look. I looked over my shoulders, and Chisenga was fading in the distance. We moved further and further away from the wire fence until Chisenga was no longer in sight.

We squeezed through the crowd. "We need space just for the two of us with a clear view of the Masasu band," Mwila said. We found a small space on the east side of the Club though it was not well lit.

The band began to play a new song on a familiar rhythm. Mwila pulled my arm and flung it around her waist, her eyes sparkling. My heart pounded as she spun and threw her arms around my neck. Now her face was on a level with mine. She looked me in the eyes and smiled. Locking her fingers behind me, she squeezed me to herself and pushed me side to side. Eventually, I got into the beat. The rhythm was slow, and her movements were deliberate. She rocked me to the music of her favourite band. "You dance so magnificently," I offered my compliments.

"It's my pleasure to dance with you." She put her foot between my legs as if dancing to a Tango. She held me close, dragging her feet. I did not know how to move. I felt locked each time her foot came between my legs. "I must lead," I thought, but she led. The music paused. She paused too.

"You know the song?" I asked.

"No," she said.

"How come you dance so well to it?"

"Shh, rhythm," she shushed me into silence as the music resumed.

She put her arm on my shoulder and searched for my hand, swinging me around. I felt stiff. "How can I loosen up?" I wondered. I took a deep breath, and slowly I caught the rhythm. "It is all about rhythm," I thought. I moved in pace with her. She stepped forward, and instinctively, I moved on too. I noticed her smile. I let her hand go and held her back. I stepped forward, and she did. I was leading the dance. Then the song started to tail off. We were bound to each other, while the music was waning. I moved closer, but she broke the magic moment. Unclasping her hands behind me, she pushed herself away. "The music is over," she said, spun twice and walked away.

I never imagined she would come so close and move so far away within such a short time. I felt my hands hanging next to my pockets. For a moment, I endured a sense of confusion. I followed her through the crowded spectators. I found her away from the Club, moving beautifully to traditional music.

"I love Chamboli," she shouted when she saw me.

"I love…" I stopped myself.

"Do you know how to dance Akalela?" I asked.

"Yes." Her voice was delightful.

"Show me how," I said eagerly.

"We cannot dance here!" I yelled.

"We are already here," she shouted, pulling me by the arm inside the circle of the Kalela dancers.

The drums rolled, and Mwila smiled and put her arm around me, dragging me to join a ring formed by the dancers. Without guitars, microphones or cymbals, Kalela sounded from three big drums hanging to a pole in the middle of the dancing floor. The Zambian flag flew high. Dancers circled the pole singing *"Mwalileni! Mwalileni! Mwalileni eee!"*

"They cannot be singing *mwalileni* when there are empty shops. No mealie meal bags and no cooking oil. Where is the feast they are singing about?" I said. Her laugh was sudden and short, engaging her dimples. Mwila swung her arms a lot more with a sense of satisfaction. "They are mocking the mining company," she said, pulling my hand for a space in front of the spectators. I wrapped my arm around her, moving side to side, forward and back. We were imitating the dancers. When the dancers dragged their feet on the ground, we did the same raising dust in the process. Drummers ramped up the beating of the drums and whistles blew from the centre.

Then, there was that strange look in her eyes. She smiled. I pulled her close to me and held her tight. She said nothing. I felt the stiffness go out of my body, and I smiled. I swung her around, making her skirt swish. She was still clinging to my waist.

She leaned toward me. In a whisper, she directed my eyes towards the spectators on the opposite side. All I saw was his back. PC Mambwe was alive and well. The dog had not crushed the bones of the paramilitary man. Maybe PC Mambwe had nine lives.

Mwila tugged my hand. Through the spectators, we hurried off towards the P Section. We passed a deserted Nkote Club. We ran past Mwabonwa Tavern. The Chibuku window was closed, and the crowd was thin.

We turned a corner. Around us, people were moving up and down. Some slowly, some hurrying. Then we passed a dim lamp-post: a boy and a girl, embracing. We walked in silence, hand in hand.

Suddenly, the mine alarm was wailing. It was nine PM, and we disappeared in the empty streets of the mine compound.

Chapter 19

The next day, the tailors, watch and shoe repairers were not there again. Even if they were there, they could not retrieve their machinery and tools from the shop. I could see sewing machines, boxes of clothes, toolkits of glue, hammers and pieces of rubber all heaped in a corner inside Fyonse General Dealers. The shop veranda was quiet. It was another day almost gone without trading in the mine compound. The notice on the door was still in place: no mealie meal, no cooking oil, no sugar, no bread and no milk. The list of shortages was growing.

I started getting anxious when Mwila did not show up at the shop. It was getting past three PM, an hour late. I wondered if she had changed her mind, which was unlikely when the Little Chiefs Football Club were playing. I was eager to watch Mwila's childhood team. Fans from the M Section were coming out in droves to watch their idolised Little Chiefs. They filled up the Kalukungu Road, singing and chanting. They beat drums, shook *ifisekeseke* and sang to intimidate the opponents from the P Section. It was the semi-final match of the under-fourteen championship.

It seemed as if everyone from the township was going to Mogadishu Stadium.

Fans came to the shop.

"Do you work here?"

"No," I responded.

"Why has the shop not opened?"

"Is there anything to sell?"

I looked at the notice, saying nothing.

"There's no cash in the township!"

"It's because of government tax!"

"The price of copper has gone down!"

"Nonsense."

More visitors came and went.

"It is the mismanagement of minerals."

"It is because of debt."

"Interest rates are too high."

"It is because of corruption."

"It is because of colonialism."

"It is the hand of fate. We Africans are meant to suffer."

I suppressed the urge to rant.

"The devil has a hand in it. Life was too good for miners, and the devil was not happy."

"It is the will of God. If he wants us to be like this, who are we to say anything."

I reserved my opinion.

"Where is Mr Phiri? Has he sewed my dress? I have a wedding to attend."

"I came to collect my shoes."

"I need a watch repairer."

"Can you see how skilled she is?" said a man proudly pointing at a woman. She was engrossed in her knitting.

"I think she's expecting." I finally broke my silence.

"Mukuba Corporation will not register her child if that's her seventh." He said. In that instant, I realised something. "This man here is Hector," I thought. And an immense number of things passed through my mind. I considered what to say and what to do, but I could not find anything. My eyes travelled with the woman as she passed the shop.

"I have never heard of that," I said.

"I got it from training." He said his eyes followed the knitting woman.

"Her child will not be born at J Clinic!" he said. My eyes narrowed as the words sank in.

"Not even at a maternity clinic? There's one in P Section," I said.

"No," he said.

"Why?"

He shrugged his shoulders, and a long silence followed.

"Do you remember me, Lumba?" He smiled and stretched his arm. I took it.

Before I could talk about the cartons he had in the L Section, Hector said, "I coached you in the under-fourteen football team, and then you disappeared. I never saw you again until last week."

"Ah! Coach. Coach Hector!" I exclaimed.

"Have you stopped coaching?"

"I was on a mining course. Zambia Institute of Technology."

"Are you going to be a mine captain? Are you moving to the other side of the mineshaft?"

He shook his head, "Unless the rules change, the

owners of the mining company come with mine captains from abroad."

There was a pause. Hector tapped his feet. Somewhere in the compound music was blaring away at some party or from the Club. "The Masasu band will be playing the whole night tonight. No one will be sleeping in the mine compound," said Hector.

"The weekend is here," Hector added, pointing at a crowd. Groups of young men and women milled up and down the road.

"Yes, it is always like this on Saturdays and Sundays. People have time to move about the street," I said.

"And to dance and watch football," he said. "Now, no money and no supplies," He continued.

"Yeah," I said wearily, troubled by the cartons he had in the safe house. "Was it Hector or Micky and his market vendors who started the riots?" I wondered.

Gesturing to the noise from the stadium, Hector stepped off the corridor, and I followed him.

"Did this man loot Fyonse General Dealers? Could he have started the riots?" I was afraid to ask him the questions.

At last, we faced the stadium. And Hector said, "A lot of township children stopped coming to play football when mine captains erected an asbestos fence around the ground and began to charge for entry fees. Talent is wasting away. Just like Melody in Wusakile, this stadium is a nursery for the Nkana and Mutondo Football Clubs. Even our arch-rival team Power Dynamos benefit from this ground." I nodded without looking at him.

"I left the stadium from this gate before the paramilitary

began to fire tear gas canisters." I began to say. "When did you get out of the house in the L Section?" I continued, but there was silence. I turned around, and Hector was not in sight. Surprised, I began to search for Hector, terrace after terrace, moved up and down. I could not see him.

Then I came into view of well-dressed men in black suits, white shirts and black ties, dancing around to the sound of bongo drums. A crowd of cheering people gathered around the dancers.

"*Imbeni*," said someone pushing to the front of the audience. The slow and low drumbeats began to pick up speed and intensity. The feet of the dancers matched the pace of the music. The drummers raised the tempo of the beats further and ruptured into a deep crescendo. Whistles blew, and the choreographed moves followed. I thought more than a hundred residents descended from the terraces. They gathered around Imbeni dancers, huddling on the playing field, pushing, and shovelling to watch the spectacle, cheering with energy and excitement.

Eventually, the drummers slowed down. And the dancers slowed too. They stopped whistling and began to sing in praise of the Honourable MP and the Chief Mine Captain. They thanked the two men for their services to the community. However, this did not last. The words of praise changed to lyrics of reproach. "Where are the free pints of milk for the children? Where are the free exercise books for those that go to school? How shall we educate the next generation? And now the misfortune that befell schools is hanging on the stadium," they sang.

"What are they singing about?" My heart missed a beat,

realising it was the voice of Mwila. Her gaze met mine. She did not flinch away as other girls would have done.

I moved close to her until we were toe to toe. "I was waiting for you at the shop," I growled. But she shifted her gaze to the man next to her. She motioned her arms to keep the man talking. "The mines are planning to sell the stadium." The man said, ignoring my presence.

"Why?" she asked.

"Greed," he said, spreading his arms around to emphasise his point.

"I met Hector!" I whispered. "He is somewhere here! Remember the man accused of looting. He's here." I tried to cut in the conversation, keeping my voice low for Mwila's ears only, but she did not pay attention. She took a few steps from me. "I was with Hector!" my voice rose. Mwila was quiet.

Pointing to the pitch, the man said, "The lime has faded, and the lines on the pitch have greyed out. The nets for the goalposts have holes in them, which is embarrassing for the biggest mining corporation in the whole world." My attention shifted from Mwila to the man in front of me. Whether he was exaggerating the position occupied by Mukuba Corporation on the mining company world rankings, I would not know. When he became specific, I began to think he may have been telling the truth after all.

"The Anglo-Americans expanded the production at the mineshaft and exported huge amounts of copper. By 1969, the gross domestic product in Zambia was ahead of Ghana, Brazil, Malaysia, Turkey, South Korea, Kenya, and South Africa. So, where has the money disappeared?" he said, his eyes met mine for the first time. I nodded.

"I am the patron of the Imbeni cultural dancers." He extended his hand, and I shook it. He smiled. I wondered if he wrote the songs that mocked the Chief Mine Captain and Honourable MP.

Then the drums stopped beating, and the patron said to Mwila and me, "Can you help me roll the drums to the grandstand?"

"Yes," Mwila and I spoke in unison.

He pulled from the pocket two lanyards, "Put them around your neck; otherwise, the Boys' Scouts will not allow you access to the grandstand," he said.

I looked at Mwila and found it hard to believe that she was the same person I danced with last night. Who could understand Mwila? But I needed to talk to her. Moving close to her, I said, looking at her again, "Hector is somewhere in the terraces." She did not acknowledge me, walking towards the drums.

My instinct told me it was her usual moods. Whatever caused her far away, deep brooding thoughts, Mwila was not listening to me. So, I stopped talking.

In silence, we rolled the drums and rested them on to the two front poles that supported the grandstand. Mwila and I began to tie the drums to the poles, listening in silence to the Chief Mine Captain and Honourable having a conversation.

"Are you closing the mine?"

"No sir, we are not closing the mine."

"Do you realise the catastrophe it would cause if this mine were to close?"

"We are not closing the mine. We are selling non-core assets."

I looked at Mwila to see the reaction, but she avoided my eyes. I pushed the lanyard around my neck, trying to look official.

"What you are calling non-core assets is essential to the survival of my constituency. It is your responsibility, Chief, to maintain the stadium and other township facilities."

"We will not allow the stadium to close. We will just find new owners."

The Chief Mine Captain leaned forward. In a panic, we stood up and pointed at the unoccupied terraced seats in the grandstand. The Chief Mine Captain reached out to the table and emptied the contents of the soft drinks into two glasses that were in front of him and offered one to his guest.

"Now we need to keep order in the township."

"I have asked PC Mambwe to meet with me here. He has instructions from me to keep the township calm."

"We have the money right now to take over the emerald mine."

The exchange went on. Worried PC Mambwe might recognise us fumbling with the drums; we left for the seats up in the terraces.

Buteko leaned back, resting his elbows on the arm of the chair, looking up into the sky occasionally. The two men drank, emptying the glasses not minding what seemed to me thirsty and hungry people around. The Chief Captain and Buteko seemed indifferent, and I felt angry. At that moment, I began to accept the Chief and his host were not going to fulfil the things the *mbeni* dancers wanted. Descent wages for miners. School supplies. Better facilities for the compound.

Just as we took our seats, I heard the dull thud of heavy boots. PC Mambwe rumbled on the terraces. "He must have seen us all along," I said to Mwila.

After a long while of awkward silences, Mwila spoke in the usual way. "He is coming after us."

PC Mambwe laboured to lift himself from one step to the next. "For a military man, PC Mambwe needed to shed off some weight." I thought. "Did he need to carry his baton, and the teargas canisters around his waist everywhere he went?" I said, dreading him as he moved up step by step. "Yes, a policeman is meant to be feared—his handcuffs, big broad belt, his heavy boots, his teargas canisters!" said Mwila with a tone of sarcasm.

I wondered what he would do with both his masters in the stand. He reached me and shouted, pointing, "Move!" I ignored him. "Move…move Lumba!" he yelled, panting for breath.

In a split second, I felt a large hand take me by the scruff of the neck. I resisted, and PC Mambwe yanked me by my shirt and pushed me aside. Mwila breathed hard. I dropped my gaze to the canisters dangling on his waist, and I moved a few steps away.

While I was inwardly venting my wrath on him, PC Mambwe had settled himself in the grandstand. Then in the most cheerful mood possible, he turned around to Mwila, "Are you okay?"

Mwila looked at me with sympathy. Then she offered him a painfully polite smile, "Fine."

"Which team are you supporting?" he asked. Mwila did not respond. "Sanctary?" Mwila gave him a look.

Applause erupted as Sanctary Football team lined

up against the Little Chiefs. Rising, Mwila looked at me, gesturing me to stay put. She kept clapping for her team, the Little Chiefs. The paramilitary officer tried to stand up but struggled. He tried to rise again and gave up and decided to remain seated.

The whistle blew, and the spectators lowered themselves to their seats. Mwila hesitated to sit down. PC Mambwe took off his cap and whipped his face with the back of his hand. Then he called above the noise of the stadium, "Mwila! Mwila!" I wondered how PC Mambwe knew her name. Mwila kept standing. "Sit down!" shouted PC Mambwe. Mwila instead decided to move to the lower terraces. PC Mambwe followed her. I was right behind the paramilitary officer.

"Get out of my way?" she yelled. A small crowd formed. PC Mambwe looked agitated and wanted to touch her but stopped himself.

"I have been looking for you," he said, "I want to know why you have been hiding." Mwila shrugged her shoulders.

"What do you want from me?"

"You tell me."

"Tell you what?"

"You ran away last night. You are not going to run away this time."

Frowning, Mwila folded her arms. I stepped back from the circle of spectators pondering on what PC Mambwe had just said. "Did he follow us last night?" I wondered. I began to suspect he was following me today and saw me with Hector. "But why is he not talking about Hector? Doesn't he know Hector is somewhere here? Has he come for Hector or Mwila?" I wondered.

"I don't know what you're talking about," she said harshly and loudly.

"Where are the market vendors?" he yelled.

"What market vendors?" she rebuffed. I thought her voice was stronger now.

"I got intelligence. A lot of people saw you with the market vendors. All I want to know is where they are?" I suspected PC Mambwe did not have information on Mwila, and I moved back into the ring and stood next to her. And I began to apportion blame for the troubles in the compound. "It is either of the two men in the grandstand or both," I thought. I was not considering Micky and the market vendors anymore. Not even Hector.

"I do not know what you are talking about?" she said without showing any signs of nervousness.

"Those men are dangerous. They crashed a wheelbarrow into the Chimanga Changa truck. They dragged the mealie-meal off the truck and set the lorry ablaze. We need them for arson."

Silence hung everywhere. The crowd murmured, and Mwila showed a puzzled face. I knew nothing about the lorry getting burnt and wondered if this was a trick for PC Mambwe to get Mwila to confess. PC Mambwe took a step forward, and my stomach lurched, but I forced myself to be calm. He came close to face Mwila.

"You got the wrong person. I do not know what you are talking about. I need a toilet," she shouted and walked past the paramilitary man. I loved Mwila even more for the strength I did not have. Without even knowing it, I was beginning to stand up with Mwila for the little belief I had.

PC Mambwe folded his massive arms across his chest,

looking at Mwila as she disappeared behind a terrace. For the first time, I felt sorry for PC Mambwe as he stood awkwardly. However, I did not dwell on him for a long time. Quickly, I ran after Mwila. But soon I realised I could not get inside. I stood outside and waited and waited and waited.

Chapter 20

It was four o'clock on Monday morning on the eighth of December 1986. There was not a cloud in the sky. The moon was full, and the stars filled up the sky, revealing how early in the morning it was. I was not surprised there was a queue at the shop as I would not be the only one in the compound to have heard the news.

"Did you also hear Fyonse General Dealers got maize-meal bags today?" said a man in front of me.

"Yes," replied his colleague.

"But only one shop got the mealie meal?"

"It's a favour for the deal!"

"What deal Champion?"

"The emerald mine."

I leaned forward, although I did not need to. The men were loud enough for everyone on the queue to hear.

"How come Mukuba Mining Corporation has the money now?" The man looked at me. I shrugged my shoulders.

His peer answered, "Remember champion, the bible says for where your treasure is… there your heart is also!"

his friend completed the quote. I wondered if it was a proper use of scriptures.

The two men looked inside the shop. Curiously, I peeped through the glass window, and I saw a clock. It was a few minutes before five AM.

The clouds from the east began to turn from total darkness to light blue. Dawn had set in, and the queue started to get longer at a faster rate than before. The alarm went off at five o'clock from the underground mine.

"And that is the last alarm we would hear from the underground mine."

"I know Champion the mine will be operating on care and maintenance basis."

"Chief Mine Captain is reducing the number of miners."

"Are you safe, Champion?"

"I got out yesterday at nine PM. I am not returning. And you?"

"I was out at five PM yesterday. Not going back."

"Champion, I can not believe what has happened to our compound."

"Tell me about it, Champion."

"It is as if bakeries never delivered fresh bread on this corridor."

"Yes, Champion. When the five AM alarm sounded, on my way to work, I would see Mbukulu and Acropolis bakeries delivering supplies on the shop corridors."

"I know Champion. The shop owners had not opened the doors at that time."

"Dairy Produce Board delivered fresh milk on the shop verandas too."

"All companies did the same, Champion."

"And I would pick up my fresh milk and bread from the corridor and left the money in a box outside the shop."

"Champion, I did the same. No need to queue up. I would leave copper and silver ngwee coins, and I would collect my breakfast on the way to work."

"No one stole the deliveries or the money, Champion."

"Yes, Champion, when shop owners arrived at seven AM, delivery vans had left by then."

"Champion, now the mine alarm is wailing and we are queuing up."

"Because Mbukulu bakery has not delivered this morning."

"I know. It is because Mukuba Mining has delivered us on the corridors."

"Ah, now you are talking Champion. We are commodities."

The men paused when the alarm stopped; the echo was tailing off slowly. I turned towards the mineshaft gazing at the wheels as they slowed down and came to a complete stop. I looked up and saw the sun's rays had broken through the clouds.

"Where does this queue lead to?" The voice was of Hector, and I turned at once. He was wearing the boots with the print of Mukuba Mining Corporation.

"Mealie-meal," responded a woman fifth on the line. Immediately, I heard a noise from inside the shop. The key clicked. I was considering talking to Hector, but I was undecided what to say to him. While I pondered my course of action, Hector walked away and went towards the end of the queue. I was about to leave the line, but the flow of my thoughts suddenly stopped me: "Why did Hector disappear at the stadium? Does he want to talk to me?" There was a part in me still latching on the idea of Hector looting the lorry.

Suddenly, the door opened, and the crowd surged forward, jamming the door. The shoppers pushed and hustled. A young man tripped and fell, and a stampede ensued. The noise from the commotion brought more people to the shop. Young men arrived and pushed their way inside the shop. Women backed off from the queue.

Peter emerged from the store and forced the door shut. A name tag on his shirt identified him as a Stores Manager. With the door shut, we began to reorganise ourselves into a queue jostling for positions. I managed to secure a second position. Later, I found myself squeezed out of the line.

By seven AM, the queue was long, and the pushing and quarrels increased, jostling escalated, and voices rose. And then came the whispers, "The shop has raised the prices." "Prices have doubled!"

Across the Kalukungu Road, an officer whipped around, canisters bouncing on his waist. PC Mambwe was coming quickly towards the shop, and I began to prepare some answers for him. My heartbeat began to race, and I gave him my back.

"What's your name?" I heard his voice.

"Hector!"

I gasped. "Hector! Hector!" I turned. Hector made a face at PC Mambwe. I wondered what PC Mambwe wanted from Hector.

"Step out of the line!" PC Mambwe demanded, pointing a baton at Hector.

Hector stepped out at once. His eyes focused on the police baton that was pointing at him.

"Hands up?" snapped PC Mambwe.

Hector followed the instructions.

"March on!" commanded the paramilitary man.

Towards the direction of Asian Shopping Store, PC Mambwe marched Hector. Gradually, they faded from the surrounding crowd, and I began to worry for Hector.

Two hours passed while the door remained shut. Shoppers had not emerged from the shop. The passage of time loosened the queue and the pushing and shoving from the front eased off.

Soon, I began to see mealie-meal bags on shop corridors. Shoppers were no longer pushing. Instead, they were talking to the boys selling the maize-meal on the veranda. Then, I recognised the catholic woman. I had asked her the whereabouts of Mwila at the parish, but I did not think she would remember me. She was knitting, talking with the young men selling the bags of mealie-meal. "The bags of maize-meal have now entered the black market," she said, pointing, and this made me sad.

The sadness increased when I thought of the woman's unborn child. If the child is the seventh to be born of her, it will not be delivered at the J Clinic. It pained me. Then, a *zezela* boy, who carries mealie-meal for a fee talked something to her. Her face became sad. She walked briskly away and disappeared.

Suddenly, the front door opened ajar. Peter stuck his head out, announced awkwardly, "Mealie-meal has run out."

"Click!" Peter closed the door quickly behind him.

"Bang! Bang!" I joined angry shoppers. Kicks and fists landed on the door. Glasses rattled.

"Open the door!" we shouted. "Open the door!"

"You are admitting people by the rear entrance!" we yelled.

Peter taped a notice from inside the glass window: CLOSED. With the rise of anger, we hit and broke the glass window setting off an alarm. When PC Mambwe emerged, tear gas canisters began to explode at the verandas. The military man was running towards the shop, as we dispersed into the compound.

Chapter 21

The afternoon was steaming hot. Mwila and Chisenga sat under a mango tree, and I seated myself beside Chisenga, watching Mwila cooking. Her hair braided in mukule. She looked beautiful, and I stared at her like a fresh flower.

A pot of fresh maize and sweet potatoes was boiling on a brazier.

"Are you hungry, Lumba?" I was not aware she had placed potatoes in front of me. I nodded. Then she got up, and suddenly turned and caught me looking at her. She laughed. "Some more food," she said aloud. I agreed.

"You are so kind, Mwila," I said. "You are friendly," she said.

"Did you see the canisters?" I asked.

"Yes, Lumba. Everyone in the compound must have seen the explosions," said Mwila. She moved her stool and sat next to me. And then she smiled, and her face looked very young in her new hairstyle. She slipped her hand into mine and squeezed it. I felt the softness of her hand. I tried to think clearly and to arrange my thoughts.

"Hector has been arrested," I said.

"Hector?" said Mwila squeezing my hand. I returned the pressure of her hand, which comforted me.

"PC Mambwe got him. Hector was on the mealie-meal queue with me," Chisenga sat up and looked at me in confusion.

"Did you buy the mealie-meal?" he asked.

"Not with so much corruption going on. Mealie-meal on the black market. The Honourable MP admitted shoppers from the back door. I was furious. I joined in a near riot which brought PC Mambwe with canisters."

"Someone betrayed Hector," said Mwila.

"I saw no one accusing Hector," I said.

"Did PC Mambwe question him?" asked Chisenga.

"No."

"Was Hector afraid?"

"I don't know. It does not matter."

"It is certain someone betrayed Hector... There's no way PC Mambwe can know who to pounce on," said Mwila.

"PC Mambwe has some informers," said Chisenga.

"He has got names of suspects. Someone is whispering names to him," I said.

"Where's he now?" Mwila enquired.

"I don't know. Maybe at Wusakile Police Station."

Chisenga shook his head in disbelief. A surprising comment from Mwila broke the silence: "We have an opportunity here. The Chief Mine Captain is keen to maintain a calm compound, and Mr Buteko wants the same thing."

"Why are they keen on a stable compound?" asked Chisenga.

"So they can protect the mines. The current copper mines and the new emerald mine," she said.

"I thought they are interested in our welfare?" said Chisenga disappointedly.

"No, Chisenga. They are not interested in us. So we need to look after ourselves," she said.

"What's the plan then?" I said, wondering what Mwila was leading to.

"I know where the market vendors are hiding."

"How long have you known that?" I asked.

Chisenga and I exchanged puzzled glances. Mwila ignored my question.

"I can talk to them," She said.

"What are you going to talk about?" asked Chisenga.

"To stop the riots. They are planning a big riot."

"What do they want?" Chisenga and I asked at the same time.

"Ending the *Senta*," she said wiping a tear on her face. I looked at Chisenga. That is not what I expected. And at once, the scary machines in Doctor Beenzu's radiology began to flash in my mind. Chisenga wore a worrying look.

"I know we all want the mining company to end the *Senta*!" Mwila was looking at Chisenga and then at me.

"What if you do not find them?" I enquired.

"They owe me…owe us. I helped them escape." It was hard to judge how serious she was with this suggestion.

"What if the market vendors do not comply? What if all they want is to loot?" I asked.

"Well, Lumba, people don't just loot. They do so because they are unhappy about something."

"You have not answered my question," I said.

"We can threaten them with PC Mambwe," she said, and I turned to Chisenga in surprise.

"That's absurd," I said.

She looked at Chisenga, and then at me. Her eyes were serious. "I know," she said. Then she folded a piece of paper, and her voice changed: "Chisenga. Lumba. I promise. I will make you understand. Trust me."

Chisenga gave her a long side glance and went silent. Then he lowered his eyes. I was equally confused but did not want to bring up more discussion, which could lead to talk about *Senta*, worrying Chisenga.

Chapter 22

I ate sweet potatoes in silence, confused and upset about her little revelation. As quietness grew deeper within me, the noise in the street grew louder. A motor car passed outside. "Greeks!" I said because I needed a distraction.

"They are going to the Asian Shopping Store," said Chisenga.

"We can take a short cut," I said, and off we went.

The Greeks parked the Datsun at the entrance of the Asian Shopping Store and offloaded a new mini-soccer on the corridor.

"Here are the balls. Enjoy the game," said one of them. Quickly, Chisenga and I were on either side of the table and engaged in the game. The Greeks collected the old table, loaded it in the van, and sped off. As soon as they disappeared, Mr Patel emerged from the shop.

"A new table?" he asked.

"Yes, Mr Patel. The Greeks have exchanged it for the old one. Would you like to play a free game with us?" asked Chisenga. "I do not play mini-soccer," snapped Mr Patel, and his attention went towards Kalukungu Road. We all noticed a maintenance van that was turning towards the shop.

"I have not seen the maintenance van for many months now. Is it on a road test?" he said with a sneer in his voice.

"It does not look like it," said Chisenga.

"A megaphone on the maintenance van: That is strange," remarked Mr Patel. The exhaust at the back of the pickup-van was blowing violently, and black smoke puffed out of its end.

Mr Patel gestured, and we followed him passed huge glass window displays of sculptures. Patel's shop was far bigger than Fyonse General Dealers. Shelves ran across every wall from floor to eye level. Pans, pots and bicycles were hanging on the walls.

Indian music could be heard, and the gigantic overhead fans blew hot air. Mr Patel pointed at empty shelves, and said, "I have not had cooking oil for six months now." "I saw a lot of delivery vans a few days ago," I said. "Yes. Fire Bakery. ROP. Colgate Palmolive. Zambia Sugar. None delivered here." "Why didn't they deliver to you, Mr Patel?" I asked. "I placed an order, and they promised to deliver. I have been asking the same questions, especially on cooking oil."

I did not know if Mr Patel was exaggerating or not. I recalled women from Chamboli Market had been selling palm oil from Congo, so I took it he was right. "ROP has a cooking oil plant on the Copperbelt in Ndola. Bakeries are everywhere here in Kitwe. From Kalulushi to Chingola. How can this region run out of supplies?" Patel moaned. I moved a few steps away in case he decided to throw a punch at whoever was running his business down.

When we came to the pallets, he stopped us and said, "Look. Empty pallets. No mealie-meal for six months. It is a big shame that in the savannah grasslands, where we can grow anything, with so much sun, rain, and fertile soils, we can be suffering. We grow maize here in Kitwe, and the millers are everywhere. Now, where's the mealie-meal?" We looked around the shop in intense silence.

Mr Patel turned to face us, "A mealie-meal truck was in the compound last night and offloaded all the bags into one shop. One shop only." He let the words sink in. "I met Buteko, and I told him I would not close the shop for his stupid meeting." We turned our attention in the direction of the Kalukungu Road. The engine of the van was running.

"It's all corruption. What's Buteko doing with the mine vehicle?" asked Mr Patel. I turned in the direction of the loading bay, and it was not Mr Buteko. Instead, I saw the Honourable MP's new Store's Manager. Peter was leaning out of the van grabbing a microphone, the two speakers mounted on the vehicle amplified his voice, "I can see you inside the shop. Are you coming out?" Peter called. We stayed on and watched. Peter got out of the van. Pulling a long cord attached to the microphone, and began to shout, "Are you coming out? Can you hear me?"

"Well, let us go," said Mr Patel. He led the way to the exit frowning angrily. We came out to a pungent smell of fumes swirling on the corridor. Peter dropped the cigarette and stepped on it. He rolled the cord and stepped inside the mine vehicle. Winding the window down, he said, "You want a lift, Mr Patel? The meeting is starting soon."

"We are not going to the stupid political meeting. Buteko diverts responsibility from himself to the mining company. He always does. None of my workers would be leaving work to attend a stupid meeting," he said.

Mwila stepped forward first and got herself in the passenger front seat. Chisenga and I followed. We squeezed next to each other, and I clutched to the door handle. Without putting on the seatbelts, Peter revved up the van in the first gear, and the mine vehicle jerked forcing Mwila to tumble on Chisenga. "Do you want to kill us?" shouted Mwila. I saw Peter look at Mwila as if to confirm his intentions. Mwila pulled the passenger seatbelt, going across the three of us, and I buckled it in. Peter coughed and sped off the loading bay without the courtesy of saying bye to Mr Patel.

"What were you doing at the parish?" said Peter, smelling of cigarettes. In the brief silence that followed, my heart rate began to pick up the speed. His voice was harsh and raspy; "PC Mambwe came to the shop looking for you three."

"Where are you taking us, Peter?" asked Chisenga.

"Police station!" he answered.

"And you, Mwila? What do you have to say for yourself?" Mwila was silent.

"What were you doing at the parish?" We did not respond.

"What were you doing in the library, you two, hey?" Peter said, his gaze wandering between Mwila and me.

"Are you going to answer me!" Peter raised his voice.

My breathing was becoming hard and laboured. I regretted getting into the van and wished I had listened to Mr Patel. I turned the door handle. It clicked, and Peter sped the maintenance van. "Don't even try it!" He blasted.

"You know Hector? He is spending a night at the police station. Would you like to join him?" I heard a snarl in his voice, and I looked outside. The trees were running past at high speed. Low hanging branches breaking in our way.

"PC Mambwe and his paramilitary friends sent me to check for the market vendors. I came into the library, and I saw you two, and then you disappeared. Where are the market vendors?" he said, looking at Mwila while the van was going very fast.

"Look at where you are going," yelled Mwila. "I would rather get locked up in the police cells than be killed by you!" she said.

"Where are the market vendors, Lumba?" Peter shouted.

Despite my efforts to hold back my thoughts, my words tumbled out of my mouth, "I do not know what you are talking about," I said defiantly. I surprised myself when I realised what I had spoken.

"Do not lie to me, Lumba!" he shouted. I glanced at the speedometer. It was at maximum speed. The van veered off the road, and it came to a sudden stop opposite the entrance to the mineshaft raising dust in the process. The seatbelt whipped my shoulder.

"You get out!" Peter pointed at Chisenga.

"No." resisted Chisenga. "Get out!"

"Unless we all go out!" Chisenga was shouting.

Peter faced Mwila and me. "Father Katyetye does not trust me anymore because of you two!"

He put his hand on Mwila's wrist. "I saw you."

Peter looked outside the window. "Look at the miners strolling on the road. That is the last shift from the mineshaft. Each miner is going to his family now; a wife and probably six children. If they get a seventh child, the child is not a miner's child." He said.

"How so?" asked Chisenga, and his gaze met mine.

We jostled when a grasshopper flew onto the van and buzzed on the window in a disoriented way. Peter opened the window and let it in. He extended his hand, and the *nshonkonono* jumped on his palm. I looked at Mwila and Chisenga in amazement. Carefully, Peter ran his finger on the wings and gently put his hand out of the window in the air. The green and red grasshopper hopped about, opened its flaps, and flew away. The mood changed.

"How is your father?" asked Peter.

"He's recovering," answered Mwila.

"The priest called for his prayers. Why don't you come to the parish now?" Mwila was silent.

"Nobody else knows what you did at the parish." He continued. I looked at him, unsure of what to say. "It could be a trap for Mwila and me to confess. Can I trust the man selling mealie-meal from the back of the shop?" I had no idea.

Another group of miners walked past the van. "Those miners have spent all their working lives for the copper mine. What have they got out of it? Nothing. I got out of the job with nothing too." He said and punched his fist into the glove component, and out popped a packet of cigarette. "Smoking is a sin, hey?" he said casually.

"Don't worry. I will not smoke here," Peter said. Putting the packet back in the compartment, he turned on the ignition and pulled into the road slowly.

"I am not taking you to the police station. The cells

are full. They have arrested half of the compound." He exaggerated, his eyes rested on Mwila. "You did not tell me why you do not come to the parish. You are away at university, right?"

"Yes," she said.

"See. I have my struggles with faith. But I keep the basics close to my heart. Love the Lord your God with all your heart and with all your soul and with all your mind and with all your strength. That's salvation, right?" he said.

"Right!" she responded calmly.

"That's what was taught by the Emmaus Bible School from Luanshya," I added.

"I did the same correspondence course too. Free postage and mail delivered home," said Chisenga.

"You want to see the mineshaft?" Peter asked.

Before anyone of us responded, Peter drove the van inside the yard of the mineshaft. There was something remarkable about seeing the mineshaft up close. The entrance to the underground and the two big wheels spinning on top were imposing.

"Every day, every hour, every minute, every second, the miners search for copper from the underground. They travel the length of the Wusakile and Chamboli compounds to drill the stones," said Peter. It took a minute or two for the information to sink in, even though it was right before my eyes. Then I felt the eyes were twitching as I looked at the structure. This is it! The entrance to the wealth that brought the British to this distant country was right before me. The steel structure showed the age and strength of the mining that helped to win the wars, build cities and prospered foreign companies.

I tried to open the door. "Don't!" Peter shouted. "The van is allowed inside, but we are not. No one gets out of the van." Then, he turned off the engine. I wanted to protest, but I could not find the words. I looked out overwhelmed, listening to Peter as he explained, "The wheels are now spinning clockwise. The miners are coming out. Do you know what it means?" Peter tapped his fingers on the dashboard. The shaft alarm would be ringing soon.

But the quietness began to fall. I could hear a steady rhythm from within the soul of the compound and the mine. I scanned the faces in the van and did not get a reaction. Silence hung in the air, as we waited for something familiar. Something that we were accustomed to. Yet, silence persisted, refusing to be filled up with the sound of the mine siren, prolonging my suffering. I felt the pain of the compound without the alarm, without cash, yet with so much wealth.

Then the big wheels stopped spinning. There was a loud squeak from the shaft door as it opened. Mwila and Chisenga clapped their hands to their ears, trying to block out the squeaking sound. Peter looked on intently. The entrance remained open for a while. Then, slow and laboured footsteps emerged.

We watched them in silence as the miners went past us. In blue overalls, black hardhats, with mutton cloths around their necks the miners from the compound were marching towards the yard exit. The Chief Mine Captain pushed a button, and the slam of the entrance made one final huge noise. I reached for my ears.

"At last, the mineshaft that had served the British with the copper, and helped them become a superior power, has finally closed down," said Peter. A chilling thought went down my spine. I wondered if Peter had prior knowledge about the final closure of the mine.

"How is it underground?" Mwila asked loudly. Peter turned his head and looked at her.

"It is dark," he said.

We all looked at him.

"Why did you leave the mine?" Mwila asked Peter.

"I failed a mine test."

"A lung problem?" enquired Mwila.

Peter nodded slowly and reached for the ignition key. I gestured Mwila, and she buckled her belt. I could not tell Peter's intentions.

He pulled the van away from the mouth of the mineshaft, and the van hummed on the road. Trees went past the window at a rapid rate as the tires whistled against the tarmac. I held on tightly to the door.

"Our trip to the mineshaft did not happen. Our chats did not happen. Do you understand? If the Honourable knows anything about it, I will lose my new job," Peter said. "And one more thing. Stay clear of PC Mambwe. He does not have the loyalty of a miner."

As we came close to the library, Peter stopped the van at the Milemu forest. "Get out now!" shouted Peter. We ignored him and looked around the forest.

"This is not the library," I said.

"Look, Lumba, Honourable has arrived already. PC Mambwe is hiding somewhere nearby. Join the crowd there. Out!" his voice was not calm at all.

Reluctantly, we got out and began to run in the gravel street towards Chamboli Library.

Chapter 23

At six PM, we made it to Chamboli Library. We hurried towards the more extended block, which had three rooms. I climbed the steps at the edge of the structure and stopped on the corridor looking into the first room.

There I was sat with my fellow young children on a small desk saying after the teachers. Elephant? Elephant! Zebra? Zebra! Lion? Lion! River? River! Tree? Tree! Grass? Grass! Somehow in this classroom, our ignorance of the savannah was being transformed. The teachers were not only assisting us in making sense of our surrounding, but they were preparing us to love, cherish and protect our compound. If not, then what use was this learning? Have the blackboards peeled off in vain? Do the endless hours of algebra gone to waste? One, two, three. We were counting within seconds of entering the classroom. And soon we became proficient. But then came boredom, which numerous times led to noise making.

So, we shot glances towards the window half expecting to see Tarzan Sanka Sanka lifting *inyanji* (a piece of rail track) with his teeth or Sugar kissing a snake or Jukusesa flipping himself on one leg. Instead, a passing milkman from the Dairy Produce Board company was on his way to deliver milk to every home in the compound. Often, though, it was a postman on his bicycle to houses waiting for a Christmas card, a postcard or a letter.

All along, on a path in the view of our classroom window, township people flowed like the mighty Kafue River. They were unstoppable, swirling around the obstacles of wheelbarrows bumping around with bags of mealie meal, containers of cooking oil or basket full of vegetables. There were laughing and joyful. Children were feeding doves foot by foot behind their parents. But teachers were not letting us out to join in until an alarm wailed.

At break time, we lined up for a pint of milk and a bun. I can smell the fresh creamy milk from DPB and feel the warmth of the brown baked pastries from Supaloaf. We did not wait for the snacks to settle. We ran about the grass lawns, climbed on seesaws, swung on the swings and went up and down the slides. But nothing feels more real than one morning when we were playing *chimpombwa* ball during break time. Unfortunately, the ball crossed over the fence into the Chamboli Market grounds. "Can we get the ball back?" I had asked. "The gate is closed," came the response from a teacher. I did not argue if the gate could ever open. It turned out to be a blessing. To avoid losing balls, we would learn ball control, and no ball ever went over the fence. Little did I know the passion was growing. It was a start of training to compete in the football under-fourteen tournaments at the Mogadishu Stadium.

At this moment, I found myself gazing at a faded picture hanging at the back of the room. It showed children lined-up on the Kitwe-Ndola dual carriageway waving flags to welcome President Kaunda and his entourage. The print text revealed the destination was a minefield. Somewhere near here was a golden land. And I felt a mystical bond to a distant past because I was among the children in the photo.

Then, I turned to face the centre of the library ground. There stood a pole that now looks lonely. Flowers had withered. I wondered if the rainwater would bring the glory of the vegetation back. Monday mornings, here, at the assembly, was like all other days. We surrounded the pole flying the Zambian flag gazing at the teachers talking in a language that confused us. "Arms up! Arms down! Forward! Sideways!" we followed the instructions. Why they gave army-type commands to pre-schoolers, I could not know.

"Lumba! I have been looking for you. Have you just been standing here?" shouted Chisenga emerging from a crowd.

"When did you last visit the library?" I asked with mixed emotions.

"I have never been inside," he said.

I was going to show him the picture. But I decided the story would be too long.

"Where did you attend your welfare school?"

"At the Welfare Community Centre."

"Where?" I asked impatiently.

"In the M Section," came the reply.

"Ah—" I gasped in realisation. I had limited the scale of resources of the Anglo-Americans, and how many buildings they constructed and the number of programs they ran from section to section.

"You cannot understand then what it means for me to visit my first school," I retorted.

Chisenga was casual. He replied with a simple "well" and shrugged his shoulders. I let him stare at me as angry faces passed us going towards classroom number three. They did not stop at room one. It was an ordinary room to many, but this to me was not a hundred bricks put together by the Anglo-Americans, but it was a classroom. A place of pure love, sincere learning, character formation carrying more dreams than the night sky has stars.

"Lumba, let's go, room three is filling up!" said Chisenga naggingly, and I decided to follow him. Between my old classroom and room-three was, of course, room two. I had never set foot in it, but the dilapidation was apparent.

"This room holds stories for many women passing it," I said, but Chisenga was not paying attention as we were pushing our way towards room three. It seemed to me the women could not bring themselves to look into a vacuum of what was once a sewing and knitting room. I wanted to stop and bring back memories, but Chisenga would not understand. Meanwhile, in the recess of my mind was the pregnant knitting woman. I thought about how different the compound would be when her child would be born. What would one see on the path along the fence of the library? Would the postman be delivering letters to the compound? Would the milkman come round every morning? Perhaps no one would know the difference. As my gaze passed over the faces across the corridor, my eyes were getting moist from the pain.

"Come in quickly," Mwila called to us standing at the entrance to room three.

Chapter 24

*R*oom three was known as the library hall. Mwila, Chisenga and I squeezed inside the overcrowded room. It was filling up with a breathless expectancy in the air.

"The priest is saying something," said Mwila pushing around. "Our prayers are with the victims of the looting. Lord, the God of mercy and grace, grant peace to our township. Guide our member of parliament, Honourable Mr Buteko, and the Chief Mine Captain of Mukuba Mining Corporation. Help them lead the compound through love and the desire to please you. May they lay aside all selfish interests. Grant that they seek to improve the conditions of living for all who live in Chamboli and Wusakile mine townships. So, may your kingdom be established here in the compound to the glory of your name. In the name of the Father, the Son, and the Holy Spirit, Amen." Father Katyetye completed the prayer. Seeing hands pressed together in prayer was agonising for me. I turned my gaze to the floor.

The "amen" echoed through the hall as the crowd jostled for positions in a parked room. There were a lot of people on the windows that could not get in the building. Father Katyetye handed the microphone to the Honourable Mr Buteko. I had no idea if they had sung the national anthem.

"Stop the sale of the stadium. Stop selling mealie-meal from the back of the shop. Stop the sale of the emerald mine," chats echoed in the hall.

"Today, Mukuba Mining Corporation has run the last shift. The Chief Mine Captain briefed me Mukuba Mining Corporation has been losing money and cannot continue running the underground mine," said the Honourable. I looked at Mwila.

"The price of copper has plummeted on the world metal market," he continued. "And we know whatever happens at the copper market affects this community and the country. We are a resilient community that supplied copper to the British to fight the Germans," he said with the sense of pride. "We are an extension of the Mukuba Mining Corporation. The problems at the mines are problems for the compound. As a result, we are all feeling the pain. Commodity shortages, unmaintained housing estates, retrenchments—." He paused. The hall was silent.

"Two weeks ago, Hector drove a wheelbarrow into a lorry carrying mealie-meal bags, causing the worst looting we have ever experienced. The troublemaker with his friends stole the bags and ransacked shops. To maintain order, I hired the Zempya Security guards. With the help of PC Mambwe, we have apprehended the man," said the Honourable with a sense of victory. He gave a huge fake sigh of relief, irking the audience, as a considerable noise erupted at the back of the hall.

"Market vendors," Mwila whispered to me pulling me along.

"Where are you going?" said Chisenga.

"Stay here, Chisenga. Look out for PC Mambwe," said Mwila.

Mwila and I moved to the back of the hall.

"What's going on here, Micky?" said Mwila through gritted teeth. I was standing next to her.

"I came to listen to the talk," he responded.

"No Micky. You must go away!"

"They cannot recognise me," said Micky in black shades and a woollen hat. He seemed consciously avoiding looking at me.

"I will not help you again," said Mwila.

"Shh," he muttered.

Mwila took a deep breath and spoke to him, sternly, "You must run."

"I am not going to run," he responded.

"Are you planning to loot again?" Mwila asked.

"I did not loot the Chimanga Changa truck," said Micky.

"Looting is not a better way to protest," said Mwila.

"I have heard that before. But listen Mwila. There is no better way to protest."

"What good does looting bring?" she said.

"You should ask why Buteko and the Chief have loosened PC Mambwe on the compound?"

"It is because of looting."

"You are not getting me. Why does the Chief want a peaceful compound when he has caused chaos?"

onsense!" shouted everyone from the hall.

ey forced our hand, and there is nothing we
.."

d so, are we stuck in our land?"

 not like that kind of talk."

ere is Hector?"

tor is a dangerous man. He started the riots. He
uck on fire."

tor was fighting for us. Hector is a fellow township

we going to let down our own?"

tor! Hector!" the crowd chanted and stormed out
. My eyes travelled around the room and rested
He was smiling, and I did not know if it was for
e of starting the riots.

She clenched her teeth, "You must go away. Looting shops is not a game. It is a serious matter."

"No!" he said emphatically. He looked defiant.

"You must go somewhere they cannot find you like Ndola, Chingola, or Mufulira. I do not care. You need to go to another big town. Somewhere they will not think of, and if they did, they would not find you," she said breathlessly.

"I am staying right here. The police have got the man they are after. They will not keep looking."

"You have caused an innocent person a lot of pain. You know Hector is innocent, and others know that fact too."

"I have been hiding alone all this time. PC Mambwe has not found me. Why should I run?"

He leaned against the wall and removed his hat.

"Did you speak to Mr Phiri?" he said. Mwila nodded solemnly. Her face was tense.

"Has he resolved his medical claim with the mines?"

"No." Mwila shook her head.

"You see," Micky said emphatically, "They will never pay him."

Mwila had no words to say. She looked around.

"You must run away. If you do not, I will tell the police where to find you," Mwila threatened him, and I cringed.

Micky ignored her, "Tell me you saw the machinery and equipment."

"What equipment?"

"Excavators, loaders, trucks belonging to Mukuba Mining Corporation. They are operating at the emerald minefield?"

"There was no such machinery."

"You did not reach the emerald mine? You did not go to Shombe Malakata, did you?"

By the expression on her face, Mwila wasn't enjoying the conversation. Whatever ideas she had to expel Micky and save the compound was not working.

"You must run away now. Peter knows about you."

"No one knows anything."

"He was hiding in the church library somewhere. He heard you. He knows." Mwila looked at me. Anxiety short up in me. I was tensing up.

"Mukuba Mining has moved machinery, tools, equipment to the emerald fields. I have seen the machines. I was there," insisted Micky.

"That's not true," said Mwila.

"The equipment is everywhere on Shombe Malakata Road and the emerald minefields," sputtered Micky beating his chest.

"I went there. Yes, you are right. I saw the equipment!" Mwila said a bit too loud and immediately looked away from Micky. I noticed a few faces were turning our direction. I smiled, pretending the shout did not come from our group. Luckily, the gazes turned to the front.

"I went. We went." Mwila looked at me, and I nodded.

"Stop the sale! Stop the sale!" the chants had resumed.

I felt Mwila would not convince Micky to leave the compound. I decided that we join Chisenga at the front. "Well, let us go. He's adamant." Slowly, we dragged our feet towards the front. We squeezed in the crowd amidst the shouts urging the Honourable MP to keep the mine open.

"Order, order," yelled Mr Buteko.

"What do you want to say?" t
man in the crowd.

"I have been thinking hard. O
independence. They did not get e
all. We need economic independ

"Have you got a question?"

"Our forefathers got organ
independence. That's what I am

"And what is your question

"Why can't we get
independence? We are now w

"And what does that mea

"We need to get the min
not sell mines to foreigners."

"I do not like that talk. I

"I am saying we have
without essential commod
plunders our minerals."

"Are you planning a
"No!"

"And so?"

"Is the government

"The government c
employment, and that
to sell new mines. I h
Corporation to resum
the mines will not pa

The face of M
indifference. He see
Mwila nodded to m
me what I heard w

"N
"T
could d
"A
"I d
"Wl
"He
set the tr
"He
man. Are
"Hec
of the hal
on Micky.
the pleasu

Chapter 25

Outside the sun was no longer shining. It was getting dark. And a breeze from the forest sharpened the coldness of the air. Chisenga, Mwila and I lingered at the hall, listening. I had no idea where the conversation was going. Father Katyetye and the Honourable mentioned Peter, Hector and the market vendors.

"I have learnt nothing new from the two men," said Mwila.

"Let's leave now," said Chisega.

"Did the plan work?" he added.

"No. Market vendors do not want to leave the compound," said Mwila.

"Did you threaten them with PC Mambwe?"

"We tried." Mwila was looking at me to agree, so I just nodded.

There was a short silence. Chisenga and I exchanged glances.

Suddenly, a roar. It was a sound of long wailing cries. *Umuntu! Umuntu! Umuntu!* (A person! A person! A Person!) echoed from the direction of the shops.

"What is going on?" Mwila was asking while walking

towards the noise. I followed her, but Chisenga remained at the library.

The Kalukungu Road was chocking with people running towards the shop, chanting, and singing songs in tune and out of tune. They gathered at the Asian Shopping Store. I moved in front of a mob and noticed the shop was closed. They were knocking on the glass double doors shouting, "Patel! Patel! Patel!". Others were calling out: "Umuntu! Umuntu!" I ran about trying to make sense of the commotion. I began to wonder whether this was the big riot Mwila had talked about.

"What is going on?" I asked the Zempya guard. He was pacing helplessly on the veranda, and his dog was aimlessly barking, cowering beside him. "Woof..woof woof…" The dog could not scare the mob away.

"Why are they calling for Mr Patel?" I asked. The guard did not answer.

"Why are they calling umuntu?"

"I do not know," said the guard tersely.

"There's a person in the shop who had been locked in against his will," answered a boy, looking in the shop window curiously.

Part of the mob moved to the rear of the shop. Mwila and I followed them along. Brown bricks, a small locked door, and a little burglar barred toilet window greeted us. Finding nothing, we went back to the front of the shop to the unrelenting shouts of "Umuntu! Umuntu!" The Zempya guard was now pleading with the mob. He seemed powerless against the persistent claim the owners had left a man locked in the shop.

I moved to the front of the angry mob. "Can you please

tell your friends to stop banging on the door!" the guard pleaded with me.

"I do not know what to stop them from," I said, and I turned to Mwila. She seemed nervous.

"Open the door!" the mob shouted.

"I do not have the keys," the guard cried, dropping his head in his hands. His dog was barking. I felt torn apart. "Should I stand on the side of the guard or the people?" While I was deciding the people were banging on the doors. "Please talk to them to stop!" he pleaded again, his dog on the leash. I stared at the dog and memories of its teeth threatening to bite me, came flooding back.

"You unleashed your dog on me the other day, didn't you? Didn't you call me a looter? Now, you want me to control the situation!" I shouted.

A crowd was growing around us, and I became nervous. But I was overwhelmed with guilt too. I felt I could not stand by and not try to protect the property of a man I have known for many years. Confused, I turned around. Mwila was not anywhere in sight. The loading bay was choking. I searched for Mwila among angry faces that covered the entire length of the Kalukungu Road. Disappointed that I could not find her, I returned to the Asian Shopping Store determined to help Patel this time. When I arrived at the front door, the glass windows were rattling. I stood next to the guard. "Where is the alarm button?" I asked.

"Why do you want the alarm button?" asked the Zempya guard suspiciously.

"We need to call for help," I shouted. The guard looked confused and blew a whistle. Swiftly the township people pushed themselves towards the door, chants subduing the whistle and scared the guard out of the way. The Zempya guard turned and went to the back of the shop. Almost immediately, a security alarm began to ring.

More security officers arrived with barking dogs. The crowd was defiant, but I was scared. The scuffle was unrelenting. And when the mob knocked the door down, everything around me seemed unreal. It was a scary scene. The glass door smashed into pieces. Tens of angry township people rushed inside the shop. Some fell at the entrance, and more pushed their way inside the shop. They ran away with cash registers, kwacha notes and ngwee coins, and I moved away hopelessly from the shop. I remembered the free games of mini-soccer granted by the Greeks. I felt despondent.

The people took anything they could lay their hands on. The shelves came crumbling down. Metals from the frames and sculpture fell in the aisles. "Umuntu! Umuntu!" The loot spluttered on the shop corridor. The balls from the mini-soccer tables spattered about on the floor. I started to hear different chants, "Zampe! Zampe!" (Free for all! Free for all!). The fluorescent lights blew off, and the corridor became dark. I hurried away from the veranda and stood at the loading bay.

The sky was cloudless, and the moon was shining bright. I felt my hand grabbed. "I have been looking for you," she said urgently. "I looked for you the entire Kalukungu Road." I held Mwila tightly.

The mob began to leave the dark verandas, heading towards the Fyonse General Dealers. Mwila and I, hand in hand, followed the crowd. The security guards were chasing the people away. Their dogs were barking so loudly, but the unrelenting mob surged on. Mwila and I stood at the Housing Office, a reasonable distance from the corridors and watched everything unfold. I was not sure I was willing to try and save a politician's shop having failed to protect Patel's shop. I was not even sure that my sentiments were right. So, I kept them to myself.

The mob pulled down the grill doors and smashed the windows. Broken pieces of glass flew about on the verandas. The angry residents knocked the doors down, got inside the shop, and took away bags of the mealie-meal and containers of cooking oil. I looked at Mwila. Her mouth was open in disbelief, "I cannot believe Peter now. He closed the shop telling us the mealie-meal was all gone! He was lying to us!" I said. "There was a notice for no cooking oil." I continued. Mwila was silent.

Hopelessly, we watched mealie-meal and cooking oil spilt over the corridor. A security alarm went off. Another one sounded. The whole mine compound was covered with every tenor of sounds of sirens. I was expecting the corridors to clear, but instead, the alarms brought more and more people to the stores. The electric wires dangled from the fluorescent lights. They swung in the winds and sputtered and "pop" a fire ignited.

More and more township people were arriving. I wondered if some came to look at the burning shops or at the looting that was going on. There were as many people on the road as in the shop veranda. I saw Zempya Security guards running about on the shop corridor, moving the crowd from the ablaze. The fire was so fierce now that I could feel the heat as we leaned against the wire fence around the Housing Office.

And then I heard nervous voices of women that joined Mwila and me. They looked fearfully at the blaze, huddled together with chitenge materials over their night dresses. "*Imwe mwe bantu*! (Oh my gosh!)" they exclaimed, "The families in the quarters!" Immediately, it dawned on me that the workers for the Honourable Buteko could be on fire.

"Peter!" I exclaimed, not saying more than his name. I was afraid of facing reality. However, the women cried in whole complete phrases and sentences: "*Imwe mwe bantu!* The families are on fire!"

I began to shake, and a vast lump clogged my throat. "If only I had helped the Zempya guard," I thought. I could not stop thinking about Peter. The more I resisted, the more my mind went back to the same thought. "Peter!" I said, and I looked at Mwila.

"I do not know, Lumba," she said, her voice was cracking. She knew what I was saying even if I just called his name. Standing watching a shop burning down and not knowing if Peter was in the shop was awful. The thought that I could have done something to save Peter did not help matters. Now, it was too late. I looked at Mwila again. She seemed lost. I began to lose hope, fearing Peter was not in the crowd; otherwise, he would have been controlling all this. I wished he could cross the road and round-up Mwila and me to take us to the police station. In my pain, facing PC Mambwe was a lesser evil than the thought of losing Peter.

"The Honourable won't be able to revamp the shop!" cried one of the women thoughtfully. "It might not burn down completely, but the smoke will have damaged everything. I am more worried about the workers that live in the quarters within the shops. They won't have anywhere to live now. I don't think they've got any family to go to," she wept.

And then I felt Mwila's hand squeeze mine. When I turned, she looked at me with a blank expression and said nothing. I thought she was communicating in silence. I could not tell if she was afraid to talk because the women could hear us.

The women by now began to shout, urging their children to cross over to the Housing Office. "Come home!" they shouted. I knew the voices would not go far in the noise, but the women kept calling. They say it is human nature to shout and gesture, even if no one is listening. So, it did not bother me to hear them wailing. "Come home! Come home!" but no one crossed the road towards us.

And then I took my eyes away from the ruins, as the devastation was too harsh to bear. I stood in contemplation in a brief silence at which point Mwila squeezed my hand again. She seemed still like she wanted to say something, but I could not think of anything to make her talk. "Shall we go home?" I suggested. Mwila merely nodded confirmation she had heard me. But she did not move.

Smoke began to blow towards us as the winds gathered momentum. The gust of wind flung the leaves and fruits on the mutuntulwa trees in its wake splashing them on the Kalukungu Road. Gradually, the clouds were hanging heavy and low, and the rumbles increased steadily in volume until they merged into a long roll which seemed to embrace the entire compound sky.

When the wind eased, the rain whipped up the corridors and the loading bays, dispersing the looters. Men, women, and the youth splashed in the water wadding the loot in the mud, the rain pounding on them relentlessly. A thrill went through me, but I resisted the urge to join in the loot. Frankly, I did not know what to do. I turned to a silent dare on the face of Mwila.

Scared, I held Mwila tightly. A siren sounded from a distance becoming louder and louder by the second. Teargas canisters brightened the sky red and white. Yelling and screaming, rioters scampered in all directions dragging the loot on the verandas.

Sirens were getting closer and closer. Mwila and I ran almost the entire length of Kalukungu Road towards the L Section. I could feel the buttering of the winds. The sky turned red and blue as police cars sped on the Kalukungu Road behind us.

Suddenly a van swerved around a corner. Police officers jumped out and ran down the street. The crowd scattered.

We hid behind the trees that were beginning to thin. The police cars were followed by IFA trucks, spraying the crowd with tear gas. I wondered why military vehicles came before the fire engines. By now, the firefighters would have been unrolling hoses and putting the fire out. That's how it had always been. Then it dawned on me that the Chief Mine Captain had reduced the number of fire trucks in the sale of the non-core assets. I waited in the hope that I was wrong. The fire trucks never arrived, and I despaired.

While we hid behind the trees, I heard a shout and a groan at the sound of what I assumed was a live bullet. The noise was sharp and echoed several minutes. Immediately, we came out from hiding and strode in the air filled with the smell of sulphur. The blue and red police lights intensified, the scent of tear gas fumes became strong, and the rain beat harder.

Running away from the shops, we joined a small crowd under streetlights at the end of the L Section. Mwila pulled tissues from her handbag and shared it out. Wiping the rain off, a man asked, "What's going on?"

"The residents have looted Patel's shop!" a random response came from the group.

"Hey, Champion, you're bleeding," said the man softly.

"Where?" the injured man said.

"Turn around. Can you feel anything here?" the man touched the back of the injured man.

"Not really," said the injured man.

"Something solid. I can feel something hard," said the man helping.

"Maybe a broken piece from a shelf lodged in my flesh," said the injured man. I squirmed at the thought of metal in the flesh.

"Looks like a bullet has gone in deep. Can you raise your hand?"

"Like this?" asked the injured.

"You need a doctor to look at this."

"Let us take him to the J Clinic," said another.

"That's too far. There is a maternity clinic in the P Section, a minute's walk from here. It's open 24 hours," said someone from the crowd.

Two men wrapped arms around the waist of the injured and set off towards the maternity clinic. Three men followed behind them.

"Why? Why did they loot the shop?" asked the man again between deep breaths, scanning the faces.

"Patel laughs at his customers," said one. "When customers walk in, he gets excited. Patel has charms to see through clothes."

The small crowd nodded in agreement, "Yeah."

"Customers resort to putting hands on their groins while in Patel's shop. One could never tell when Patel is at it."

Another one said, "Parents have stopped sending children on errands to Patel's shop. A child went missing six months ago, and another one month ago, and we have not seen them since. They have been put in Patel's business as juju to bring in more business for him..." It was something I had heard before. How could I not believe this man? He was repeating what elders said when they told us never to venture beyond the counter of the Indian shop. And it was always the case that I would stand on the shop veranda until customers came in.

"That does not make sense," gasped someone from the crowd.

"Patel's sculptures have been broken. They have destroyed his gods and goddesses. Those wood and Chinaware figures can see and listen to conversations. They make the shop dark and heavy. As from tonight, the gods of Patel are no more."

"I know Mr Patel. He is a good man. The sculptures are mere decorations. They are not his gods. Even if they were his gods, what does it matter to us?" Someone moaned.

"Nonsense. Everything you are saying is nonsense. Patel is a victim of the Honourable Mr Buteko who told the gathering this afternoon that he had apprehended a man that drove the wheelbarrow into the Chimanga Changa mealie-meal lorry." He paused.

"Hector!" shouted someone.

"Yeah, Hector. The people got angry. Word spread that a man has been locked in a shop against their will. They went to Patel's shop, shouting, "Umuntu! Umuntu!" The demonstrators broke down the doors. When the mob did not find anyone in the shop, they started looting. They were not rescuing anyone or shouting umuntu anymore. They were calling for zampe. It dawned on them they had ransacked an innocent man's shop. It was too late. Confusion ensued. Some went to the Honourable's shop and in anger broke down the shop." He paused and looked around. His gaze met mine. I felt a sense of guilt, holding Mwila's hand tight.

Canisters started to explode close to us. The only saving grace we had was that fresh wind from the forest quickly pushed the gases away. Later, we also got relief from the rain that was now easing off.

At full speed, an ambulance wailed towards us and turned to the maternity clinic. We hurried to the clinic and saw a nurse and another medic carry the injured man on the stretcher and put him into the ambulance. Reversing the ambulance into the street, the driver turned on the siren and sped towards the J Clinic.

"I hope the man is okay," said Mwila quietly.

"Mwila, can I ask you something?" I looked at her.

"Well, you can ask, Lumba." She gave me a look that caused me to sweat in my palms and elevated my heart rate. I felt it was a perfect opportunity to get it off my chest, and yet, all I could do was stutter. "Remember…Remember?"

"Yes?" she raised her arms, and I folded mine. Then I calmed down.

"It's just the two of us now. Everyone has gone away," I looked into Mwila's eyes.

"You are scaring me, Lumba," she said. I watched the flies circling the lamp, as the rain had stopped falling.

"Well, you remember our dance at the Nkote Club."

"What about it?" She frowned.

"Mwila," was all I could say.

"Yes," she purred.

"There is something pure in the way you do things. You have kept me on edge. I am just honest here. Mwila, I love you."

I stammered wondering what came out of my mouth. Mwila held my hand tight, and her face relaxed. She grinned and pulled me away, and I lifted my eyes to the moon in the cloudless sky. The moonlight was bright and shone on her face. I moved closer, looking into her eyes. Her face was like a full moon; calm, unfathomable and yet pleasing.

"Are you asking me out?" she asked. I nodded, nervous to know the answer.

Chapter 26

J walked down a gallery and on the walls were items. I could tell that they were made from local copper because the stamp showed Mukuba Mining Corporation. Various minerals were mined at the underground mine, but copper was by far essential to Mukuba Mining. It brought in the foreign currencies to both the company and the country. I was not surprised that I was not the only one looking at the items. Men and women stood in the hall. They were all dressed in suits. It seemed to me that they were guests for they manifested typical guest behaviour; over-polite and speaking in calm tones. Then they turned facing where I was standing. I noticed that the men wore watches made of polished copper. Their women adorned their necks with emeralds from the new mine on the Shombe Malakata Road.

Something glittered in front of me. "This way," one of the guests said. They looked at each other and turned towards the hallway. They walked fast, and I followed behind them. One side of the wall was covered in paintings from the floor to the ceiling showing scenes of a variety of sunrises. Soon, I realised they had the same background—the mineshaft. I stopped at once.

It was not only sunrise paintings that I saw but also paintings of sunsets. There was one half-round sun on a clear blue sky over the Nkote Club. The pictures of sunsets did not have the mineshaft. Instead, I saw the Milemu forest. It was no longer the green forest that I knew. The eucalyptus trees were far between, dry and withering. "This is the place where the name Chamboli came from," I said shivering. The termite mounds were as hard as a rock. I looked closely, and I could not see any insects flying. There were no *nshonkonono* or *inswa*.

My heart sank the more I looked at the painting. The foliage was brown, almost black. The Kamatemate River was dry. The banks that grew gardens of Christmas plants and purple reeds had yellowish mud. So, I moved from painting to painting to know why the river that once watered the forest had dried up. I noticed the colours of pebbles on the sides of the river were showing layers of decades of pollutants. There was neither swimming nor fishing. Even if it rained and water-filled up the river, it would not be wise to catch the Bwenga fish and eat it. Then I realised tears were dripping down my cheeks. The guests were far away from me. They did not notice me crying. How could they see me when they were looking at the sunrise? So, I went to meet them. I was determined to show them my tears and show them the sunset.

We met between the sunrise and sunset paintings, where stood a picture whose dimensions were the smallest of them all. The guests seemed astonished to see this painting. I saw their mouths open as they gazed at the depiction of a reddish earth anthill like an igloo surrounded by small trees scattered over an expanse of green grass. It was labelled "The Savannah". It was the only painting with a name. "Oh, what a sight!" I sighed, and my tears dried up. More and more guests gathered around it. I heard "the Savannah, the Savannah" until the gasps pierced my ears to the point of pain. Gradually, my eyes were closing. When they were completely shut, a distinct fragrance emanated from within the building. I stood still for a moment, trying to remember what the burst of aromatic smell was.

Slowly, I began to open my eyes, and I could see Mwila silhouetted on the savannah. In an impulsive motion, my feet firmly planted on the floor, my neck turned degree by degree towards a slow smile that was broadening on her happy face. On her earlobes were studs of shiny gemstones. When she touched the necklace, the stone on her cleavage began to glow, lighting up her purple top that clung to her narrow waist. I saw her thin eyelashes blink, exposing sparkling eyes. Then Mwila walked away from me saying nothing.

I watched her steps. She straightened her tight skirt, walking carefully in flat shoes. One step. Two steps. And then she could not move any more. I saw colourful butterflies emerging from every corner of the gallery. They flew over Mwila's shoulders, and they travelled towards the sunlight. Now, she started to move again. I could not see her face, for she was facing away from me. So, I lowered my gaze to the large emerald on her ring finger. I recognised the stone. It was the one called the Zambian Emerald. Even from afar, I could see the deep green hue with slight bluish overtone. The emerald emitted lights like stars twinkling over a silent mine compound.

I became jealous. However, I could not be sure if I were envious of the emerald or Mwila. I held my breath. Turning around, I noticed the guests had bent their necks. They were looking at Mwila's glowing finger. "I must protect Mwila!" I said. My steps were swift as I went ahead of the guests. My gaze followed Mwila's moves.

Tired, I sat down on a soft seat opposite Mwila. Immediately, she stopped walking. The guests surrounded her and began to talk to her at once. "Where can we find this emerald? Where can we mine this copper?" I leapt from my seat in a rage and sprung across the room. Mwila took a step and raised her hand to stop me, and turned around, striding away from me towards the small painting. Every step she made was painful. My chest became tight, and my eyes filled with tears. Mwila dipped a brush in copper paint and changed the name of the painting to "The Copper Savannah." The guests gasped.

At once, a waiter dinged a dinner gong. I looked up the wall clock. I could not tell the time, and I began to struggle. Mwila walked away from the Savannah painting, and the guests followed her. "Mwila! Why did you reveal the secret?" I cried. She said nothing. "Why did you show the wealth?" She said nothing. The gemstone earrings began to glow, and the copper necklace was shining. The stone on her necklace started to glitter. Her emerald ring was glowing. When the Savannah painting radiated, the host turned off the light, and the gallery lit with bright copper.

A slow song began. The music was new to my ears. It was a mixture of the drums of the Serenje Kalindula band

and the guitars of the Masasu band. I stood still to take the tune in, watching the trees waving the leaves to the music with joy. Then I saw, the black swallows of the rainy season fly away from the trees. They chimed in the music, flying high on the high notes, and diving low on the low notes. When the cymbals sounded, grasshoppers emerged from the trees. *Inshonkonono* flapped colourful wings to the rhythm. A gentle breeze blew in through the window. The leaves of the mutuntulwa trees let down droplets of rain onto the anthill that stood at the centre of the gallery. Then the sunlight came into the gallery. It's strength and warmth affecting the termite mound, releasing a smell of warm earth. An explosion of the termites erupted. "*Inswa!*" I tried to shout but could not. Then the room became dark, and the song stopped.

"Sir, the table has been set for you," a waiter called to me when the lights turned on. Looking around, I could not see Mwila. "Sir, your table is on this side." She was pointing towards the Savannah painting. Glancing wearily, I followed the waiter to the table set for two guests. "Where is Mwila?" I whispered to myself. I touched the sides of the plates and cutlery of copper and emeralds. They were warm. I could not start to eat without Mwila, so I waited until a gong sounded from the wall clock. I looked up, and it was midnight. The guests had left. I was overwhelmed with fear.

A tap on my shoulder and I turned at once to see only an image of Bob Marley. I quickly forced my eyes to close, but I could not go back to sleep. I did not know if I wanted to go back to the dream. It was the only way to find Mwila, but it was a place of unfulfilled promises. I lay in my bed with eyes wide open and filled my mind with dreams and hopes.

Chapter 27

When my eyes could see clearly, I saw the clock on the wall showed five AM. A thunderstorm had started and got me out of bed. I looked out of the window. The sky was grey, and giant clouds were hovering over the compound. With the Savannah painting on my mind, I immersed myself into the murmuring of the rain on the roof. It sounded like the *nshonkonono* buzzing.

My gaze lifted to the streetlights, but I could not see the grasshoppers. I wished it was the sound of the *nshonkonono*, for it was the opportune time when the grasshoppers were plentiful. And I knew the *nshonkonono* flew mostly in the morning. But what exact time did they emerge?

Inswa, on the other hand, rose mid-morning or mid-afternoon. I also knew that *inswa* was part of the insect kingdom under the ground where copper and emeralds abound. For the *nshonkonono*, I knew nothing of where they came from. Do they come from the land of the jewels?

Whatever questions remained, I thought I heard the familiar buzzing and amazing flapping of the *nshonkonono*. I was ready to enjoy the sight of their flight. But there was nothing except the rain hitting on my window. I felt very lonely despite the calming showers.

I was missing something too. I tried to force whatever I was feeling out of memory. And then I looked up the clock. It was half-past five AM. At that moment, it dawned on me the underground alarm had not wailed. I began to recollect my thoughts, and dimly remembered changes were taking place in the compound. I could not be sure, and I went for the dial on my ITT Supersonic Three Band radio, tuning into the Zambia Broadcasting Services. A radio announcer described the compound for me.

"Branches of mutuntulwa trees were brought down by Chamboli residents that blocked the Kalukungu Road barricading themselves from the paramilitary police. Logs and stones heaped on the tarred road. There are scenes of wreckage, burning shops, burning vans, smashed windows, smoking canisters, broken bottles—"

I increased the volume and sat up on my bed.

"The organisers have cancelled the finals for the under-fourteen football teams scheduled at the Mogadishu Stadium. The police have arrested looters. And shortly, the Chief Mine Captain will be in the mine compound to assess the damage."

It hurt me the stories covered the burning of the buildings and nothing about the people that lived in them. I wanted to know something about the whereabouts of Peter. I felt I needed to know and that it was necessary for my peace of mind.

I patted my pockets. It was still there. Pulling out the piece of paper, I read the two words written on it; Stop *Senta*. I listened to the rain, but the inspiration did not come. Even the picture of Bob Marley could not help me remember. It was when I turned the paper over and found one word, "petition", that I recalled the text was in Mwila's handwriting. The memory of lungs with circles and crosses brought goosebumps on my arms.

I tried to clear the confusion in my mind and soften the ball that clogged my throat. I was fighting tears, staring at the piece of paper, and my heartbeat seemed to echo in the cabin. "It's not too late to tell the truth. But what truth is there to tell?" I said to myself. "What had happened to the compound could not be undone." I thought. My mind took me back to the shops.

I began to hear the shouts. Umuntu! Umuntu! And then there was the banging of the glass windows and the smashing of the glass. The memories of the spark that set the shop ablaze jumped into my mind, and my chest tightened. "How can we make amends? What would I tell Mr Patel?" I decided that confession was out of the question. "I did not owe Patel anything." I tossed the thoughts around in my head, guilty at the idea of not helping Patel or the Zempya guard. Then I worked out how to banish the guilty feeling. I folded the petition and put it in my pocket.

An engine roared, and I looked out of the window. Three men in paramilitary uniforms got out. They broke the gate down, and I pulled the curtain, turned off the radio and went under the bedsheets.

I knew from the start the cabin would be engulfed in smoke, and the street littered with tear gas canisters. I waited to hear the blustering of teargas canisters, but there was none. Instead, it became quiet. Gradually, the door was rattling. Then I heard boots stomp on the street. I listened to the whispers of voices speaking in Nyanja.

I waited and waited. "Maybe the paramilitary will knock down the door. Maybe the cabin will be swept away." I was shaking with fear and anticipation, not knowing what was going on outside. It was silent for a long time before I heard the roar of an engine again. The cabin windows were vibrating as the engine was running. The lorry drove away, and the noise faded. It was not long after when I heard another sound of the engine approaching, and the windows began to vibrate again. The second IFA pulled up in the street opposite my cabin, and the engine stopped. Doors clicked open, and boots landed on the road. I waited for the shelling of the house. There was nothing. The second IFA left the street, and the third arrived until I could not count anymore.

One. Two. Three. Fire! An explosion of canisters erupted. Through the curtains, I could see the sky turn red. "Fire!" went the shouts. Heavy footsteps echoed from outside the street. From houses nearby and far away, I heard cries. Police sirens came and went. I covered myself as if ducking the canisters. I thought of PC Mambwe pulling canisters from his waist and throwing them around the compound. I pondered if the paramilitary men were protecting the minerals or the township. I plugged off my ears from the loud noise outside.

When I released my hands from the ears, the street was deathly quiet. There were no sounds of engines and no stomping boots and no exploding canisters. Eventually, I heard a cough, a barking dog, and a voice in the distance. I got out of the covers, slowly drew the curtain and peered through the window. The scene was scary. Smoking canisters scattered about on the street. The roofs of houses were barely visible as the smoky gases covered them from view.

By mid-afternoon, the black smoke had disappeared, and the sun shone brightly. I opened the window to let in some fresh air. Then I saw three police motorcycles. They sped past the Housing Office. Shortly, a motorcade of police Belmont, Fiats, Mazda, Peugeots, and Land Rovers drove past at a snail's pace.

I turned on the radio. "The Copperbelt region police has arrived in the compound ahead of the mine managers… on a typical visit, they would have driven on the road with trees decorated in national colours. Flags would have been flying in schools and on public institutions. Women and cultural-performing artists would have been dancing. And school children would have been clapping on the side of the roads. There is none of that. They are greeted instead by broken windows, empty streets, empty markets, empty shops, deserted offices, deserted bus stops, closed schools, closed churches, closed clinics, litter, and wreckage all over. Who is to blame for all this?"

I imagined the mealie-meal bags, cooking oil containers, books, and blankets from the shops that did not make it to people's homes were floating in the water. Some of the loot would end up in the narrow Kamatemate River, churning in the current towards where it meets the Kafue River. The Mighty River would be rushing and gushing and pouring over copper-rich rocks, behind mine compounds, between the grasslands and anthills of the savannah to the Zambezi River and finally to the Indian Ocean.

Then the grasslands of the beautiful savannah would be polluted. Toxic canisters would create unknowable pollution fused with the sulphuric acid from the mine. It would begin to rain for only the heavens cared for the compound to cleanse it of every waste, every toxin. Only the wind, the rain and the river could clean the township but who would wash the pain, the betrayal that the township people felt? I increased the volume on my ITT supersonic band and turned my attention again to the Kalukungu Road.

I looked at the traffic through a window. A mine vehicle stopped at the Housing Office, and a man got out and went inside a black Belmont with a loudspeaker on top. "I'm the Chief Commander of the Copperbelt Region Police. I have with me the Chief Mine Captain of Mukuba Mining Corporation. Property in the township has been vandalised. I will deploy more paramilitary officers and put the township under a curfew. No one is allowed on the street." The loudspeaker bellowed.

The Belmont began to move. I could not hear the speakers anymore. Not long after, I heard IFA trucks roar on the Kalukungu Road, and I withdrew from the window and hid under the blankets.

Chapter 28

*M*y heart jumped to my throat when I heard his name mentioned over the radio. Not that I had not seen him taken away by PC Mambwe, but I had not expected it to come to this. A sudden feeling of anger came over me. I did not know whether to scream or not. I did not yell, but a lump blocked my throat. I let the tears that formed in my eyes drop down my face as I listened to the morning news.

"A resident of Chamboli Mine Compound identified as Hector Chanda has been charged with arson." The newsreader went on to give more details of the case. Hector Chanda! Hector Chanda! His name bounced in my mind.

I rose to the sound of chirping birds and clucking hens. The doors were opening and shutting, bringing me back to the realities around me. I looked at the wall clock, and it showed 7.05 AM. I stepped outside to a bright, sunny, and warm morning, settling down on a stool under a big mango tree.

"I have a panel of experts with me to explain the causes of and remedies to the riots." The radio announcer introduced her experts.

My neighbours were tuned to the same radio station and

were listening to the same stories. I was almost sure every broadcaster in the world was talking about my compound. I could only imagine what the Zambia Broadcasting Services, Kitwe studios would be showing on the television later in the evening, and I pulled the radio towards me.

"It is a fact that prices of minerals have plummeted on the world market. We saw last year similar protests in the United Kingdom. Miners went on strike to prevent the closure of the British coal industry. The riots have become a common way of expressing dissatisfaction with inequalities in society."

"You are confusing the right to protest and the crime of looting," argued another expert.

"You must be asking what causes looting and not if looting is a crime."

"The mine company that reaped vast profits without improvement in the processes cannot be complaining about high operation costs."

"The problem is greed. The mines have increased their profits by senseless reduction of miners, and the lack of township maintenance. They have stopped funding education and now are selling off all the facilities."

"And it is not only the mines. The politicians have become greedy too. Look at the mealie-meal that was looted from Fyonse General Dealers when the Honourable MP announced he had run out of the staple food."

"It was clear the high industrialisation of the Copperbelt region fuelled the prices of commodities making the miners demand more pay, but the owners of the mines declined to raise wages. So, the miners kept cultivated lands, mabala, to supplement their low salaries. Now this, the looting, who's to blame?"

I hated the way they called them mine owners. "Who are owners of the mine?" I asked myself. "Why not me who was born in Chamboli? Why not someone born in Wusakile? And those born in Mindolo? All the mine townships in Kitwe. What does ownership mean? We are the owners of the mines. Mukuba Mining is renting it from us." I said aloud, feeling a fire of desire. I wanted to be with Mwila. It would make me feel better if I could talk to her. I did not know whether the experts on the radio made sense. Maybe she would come up with the answer as she usually did. It would help me.

"And then the monsters stopped the subsidies pushing the prices of commodities even higher. Now, the miners are hungry and angry," the expert said.

"Which monsters?" asked the radio announcer.

"The IMF," said the expert.

"Well, we shall refer to them as IMF or International Monetary Funds," she scolded the expert.

"That's what the Honourable Buteko calls them," he said lamely.

"But not on this program," she said firmly.

"The mine owners refused to dialogue," Said another expert in what seemed like an attempt to save the situation.

The word dialogue led me to dip into my pocket and got out the petition and stared at it. Stop *Senta*. Is this all? Is this what the market vendors want? Can this stop the riots?

And then, I heard the roar of the truck and looked up across the Kalukungu Road. It was indeed a military truck full of paramilitary police. As more military vehicles roared onto the road, I felt as though I was dreaming. Has it come to this? Why did this happen? The military lorries were rumbling over broken branches.

Was this all because of the rampage on the Chimanga Changa lorry? Then a realisation illuminated my thoughts. It was everyday talk among the older patrons of the township. They said Zimbabwe had become independent. Apartheid in South Africa was on the way out. And the world wars ended a long time ago. It was all because of the riches found underground. So, I thought the minerals had the power to transform the world. "Indeed, the precious stones made the compound but failed to keep it," I concluded.

I looked at the petition. I tried to say "Stop *Senta*," but I hesitated. I heard movements, and I immediately turned off the radio. The noise was of a dog that dashed towards the gate. I heaved from the stool and kicked off the radio accidentally. Another dog barked from a distance. Suddenly, military foot stomps hurried outside in no apparent direction.

Outside the gate stood three men in military uniforms and guns in their hands. They pushed the gate, but it did not open. I fumbled to grab the radio. I managed to hook it by the aerial. I was sure the door to the house was open. When I pushed, it did not move. Looking back, I saw the men kicking the gate to enter. The dog was barking at them furiously. My hands trembled on the doorknob, and my eyes watered. "Open the gate!" the military men shouted. I gripped the knob tightly and twisted it slowly, and it turned effortlessly, but the door did not open.

I felt there was something behind the door. Sweat trickled down my neck. I pushed the door hard, and what wedged in the door moved. Squeezing myself through a narrow opening of the door, I threw the radio on a chair. I shut the door behind me, sticking the metal bar across the entrance. My body felt hot, and I was sweating profusely.

"They have come for me now. The paramilitary men got Hector. They must have gotten Mwila and Chisenga. Who told them about me? Peter? Yeah! Peter cannot be trusted." Then I recalled I had not heard of Peter since the blaze at the shop. I wanted to know what happened to the families that lived in shop quarters. I had no way of knowing except listening to the radio.

I held against the door. I heard the gate being forced open and boots stomping hurriedly towards the door. "Open the door!" they shouted. I got more and more terrified. My breath quickened as I heard the creaking of the door. I was trembling, holding onto the door. "Police. Police. Open the door." My heart pumped hard like it was determined to escape. I thought it would explode. I looked around the room, and I was ready to run, but the sitting room was as open as the pitch at the Mogadishu Stadium. There was no place to hide, and I remained where I was—scared.

"I cannot barricade myself forever. My weight could not sustain me, and I will eventually give in. Then I will be taken to prison and meet Hector. I will see Mwila and Chisenga. Maybe PC Mambwe has got the picture of Mwila, Micky and the market vendors," I thought. I wished the ground could swallow me.

Again there was the banging on the door. "We can hear you are behind the door. Stay away from the door!" a voice came from outside the house. I was getting tired and not balanced. I was now leaning on and not pushing my weight against the door. I felt I had lost all my strength. Zempya guard came to mind, and I hated him for kicking Chisenga's ribs. PC Mambwe jumped up to memory and hated him for knowing my name. I hated him for pursuing Mwila. I hated him for picking up Hector. I hated him for everything. Then fear hit me. I wondered if I had dropped the petition. My eyes widened as I put my hand in the pocket and felt it. Then my body relaxed. I looked at the handwritten note, and memories of Mwila moved me from the door.

I waited for them, not knowing if they would enter by the door or by the window. There was a brief silence that was broken by a distant siren. And then, a massive shout. "Stand back from the door. We are coming in. Three, Two, One. Stay away from the door!" And a huge bang followed. They knocked the door down. All I saw was a dark figure emerging through the door.

Chapter 29

*H*e stood in the doorway. With massive shoulders and dark eyes, he was intimidating in his red beret. "This is not PC Mambwe," I thought and sighed.

One by one, men in green military uniforms and long black boots on their feet entered the house. The dark figure pointed to the corners of the house, and his men took positions in an instant. Lowering his gun, he cleared his throat and said, "Listen, carefully! My men will comb every room, every corner of the house and outside. It is in your interest to surrender all items looted from the riots right away. Do you have anything buried in the garden or hidden away?"

"Nothing," I said calmly.

"We don't want to spend a minute longer than necessary. First, is everyone home? Any foreigner, someone who's not a Zambian; a Congolese or Senegalese, anyone?" he asked and moved about in the room. He turned his gaze at me, waiting for a response. I searched the room with my eyes and shrugged my shoulders, and I rose.

"Do not move. We are going to check your house." The soldier in red beret said. I was terrified as I watched the soldiers comb the room, pushing the furniture around and pulling down the picture of Bob Marley. They moved from the sitting room to the bedroom, retrieving shoes, tropical sandals, boots, and slippers and dumped them in the sitting room. Scowling the items, they showed no interest in any of them.

"They do not look new!" a soldier yelled. He looked around the room, studying the articles and furniture, then he shrugged and cleared his throat.

"All right, come see that?" he said.

"This is an old radio," I said.

Frustrated, he grabbed the radio from me.

"Receipt?" he yelled.

"I do not have a receipt. I bought it a long time ago."

The soldier ignored my explanation and put the radio in a corrugated cardboard box.

"Follow me," He snapped.

As I stepped outside, the rainwater took me by surprise with its strength. It splashed up my canvas shoes and spattered across my pair of corduroy trousers. My heart had already started to quicken, worrying about the destination.

I walked gingerly along the road and braved to look on the side. There it was. It looked worse than I had expected, a blackened, still smoking wreck of a shop. The roof was half-carved in, the windows were gone, and the once neat corridor, the place we used to refer to as Mr Phiri's office was full of burned debris. Even from a reasonable distance, I could smell that half-roasted mealie-meal in burning cooking-oil. It was a total ruin. I was filled with sadness seeing shops I bought sweets from lying in ashes. The shops that once overflowed with goods and supplies into corridors were burnt down. I could not understand why the home of Supaloaf Bakery lacked bread. "How can the Savannah lack mealie-meal," I thought Patel was right. I felt sorry for him.

I looked at the shop once more. Smoke was rising. "There is no way Peter could survive in this ruin," I thought.

We moved further down the street. The sun was shining on the damp ground. I walked around the rainwater that covered the roads. The grass to either side was green, the air humid. Here and there, the reeds and the flame lilies were budding. The furrows flowed like streams, letting gravel and mud from the streets enter the yards. When we crossed the Kalukungu Road, the scene was scary. It revealed broken branches, logs, plastic utensils, corrugated carton boxes, broken bottles, burnt cartridges, marooned shopping trolleys, pieces of store shelves and canisters. The air in the pathway smelt dense, itchy, and unpleasant.

I strode up to the footbridge nervously assessing the water level. A lot of water streamed down the furrow under the bridge. I wondered whether it was rainwater or some of it came from the Kamatemate River.

One thing I knew was that I had to walk carefully. If my feet stumbled, it would not only be my radio, but my whole self would be swallowed in the flow and flushed into the Kamatemate River. I took a steady step as the debris hit the bridge hard swirling about before it disappeared down in the current that would join the Kafue River to the Zambezi River.

Long and vast and empty. Street after street. It was tranquil. I could hear the buzzing sound of insects on the lamp posts. Everything looked so unfamiliar. I felt a stranger in my compound.

"Where is Mwila?" I wondered. "Could she be resisting an arrest?" And then I decided she was not. But how can I be sure? She could have told them about the parish and Micky who did not want to run away from Chamboli. Strangely, I wished Mwila was here with me.

But then I tried to forget about her. I wanted the feeling of love to go away. It felt unreal. In one moment I hated the memory of her, and in another, I missed her company. I missed the youthful brown hands. Soft and smooth.

Puddling in the clutter with my radio was her fault. But she had reasons for it. All I needed was to listen and understand. But what was there for me to understand?

Now, I was not bothered by her reasons. And it mattered less if Mwila chased Micky from Chamboli. Her little plan did not help. I felt that I acted foolishly, following her useless ideas.

Then, I listened to the noise of the boots of the soldier. I hated his stomps. It pained me he did not jump over but splashed through a rain puddle, throwing mud and water all over the place. It exaggerated the emptiness of the compound.

"Keep going!" The soldier charged at me while I was deciding where the road was dry. His voice made it worse, and I hated the plan to sell the stadium. I hated the change and did not care what caused it. I decided I did not like it.

"Turn left, cross the road, stop, turn right," he shouted commands. When I hesitated, he gestured with his gun. Terrified, I quickened my steps, joining township people carrying carton boxes. We went the same direction, escorts behind us, some were pushing wheelbarrows loaded with mealie-meal bags, cartons of sugar, and containers of cooking oil.

I looked at the streets and houses and people, and they were just streets, and the feeling that had passed over me was like a dream, unreal. We crossed another bridge

Then we walked past the Nkote Club where I danced with Mwila. I turned my head suddenly. "Yes. This place was where I felt the happiest." It was as though Mwila was there, looking at me with those black eyes and the lovely dimples. I could feel her smooth brown skin. And her teeth sparkled behind her smile.

And then I thought I would not see Mwila again. She might be hiding somewhere or had run away from the compound. The feeling was very sharp and real. Not dull and numbing. It was there, hurting. And the lump in my throat choked me. "Can someone go through love and hurt and confusion all together?" I wondered. Through my brain, slowly, I filtered real from unreal things.

It was real. The Nkote Club was deserted. Debris lay everywhere. No band. No music. I looked hard down the road but could not see Mwabonwa Tavern. I wanted to see the places where Chamboli came alive. But it was quiet.

We passed the Chamboli Library, and we were facing the market. The sight that greeted me was of the wreckage of the Chimanga Changa truck. The lorry did not have tyres, and as I stood there, I could smell the aftermath of the burning tyres. What remained of them were rims resting on the ground. I was surprised that no one in the compound mentioned the burning of the tyres.

When I went around the truck, I saw broken glass

windows. I followed the compound people who, like me, were assessing the damage. We jumped over the pieces of glass scattered near the vehicle. Rainwater was overflowing from a nearby furrow—bags of mealie-meal in the trench.

Curiously, I strolled once again around the trailer, and for the first time, I thought PC Mambwe was telling the truth. It was burnt.

"This is the lorry!" said one man who was standing near me.

"Where is the wheelbarrow?" asked another. I looked at the man asking, and I nodded, saying nothing. I noticed that everyone was asking questions, "What happened? Why did this happen? Is this the truck?" There were nods and more questions and nothing more.

I shook my head in disbelief, and my escort soldier did not seem to appreciate the gesture. All he could do was yell directions, "March-on! Keep going!"

Chapter 30

At last, we crossed the road and were in the Chamboli Market grounds. "This is where I will surrender my radio." I thought. Already I could perceive the smell of smoke and the indistinguishable sound of voices ahead. First, I saw open fires and rising smoke with boiling pots of water spurting out steam. There were officers around these fires. Cartons of Kawambwa Tea and Zambia Sugar lay by the tents. The officers descended on the packages and broke them up savagely. I watched the scene in horror, holding the box tightly.

"These men are helping themselves to the items they have confiscated from the township!" I wondered. In between making tea, the soldiers kept on throwing wood onto the fire to keep it going. A heap of wood lay near my feet. I recognised the timber as that used by market vendors to make stands for their merchandise.

"Move!" shouted my escorting officer. I followed a small crowd carrying boxes like mine. We meandered through the dark green tents that had replaced the market stalls and had extinguished the beauty of the market. I could not see the Milemu forest on the other side of the camp. The Kamatemate River that flowed near the forest was silent. Its usual murmuring and the occasional babbling and burbling was silenced. I imagined the Savannah losing trees to *Senta*, and the Kamatemate River tried up by the acidic sulphur dioxide water. Then I brought my thoughts to my immediate surrounding. Chamboli Market was now a campsite for hundreds of soldiers escorting scared people.

The recent rains had made the path wet and muddy. My feet were wet, and I stopped briefly to roll up my corduroy. We continued the long walk along a meandering pathway tangled with ropes holding the tents. Shortly, we came across a vast green shelter. A long queue of the compound people laden with boxes queued up outside the tent. Smoke billowed over the tent diffusing the bright rays of the morning sunlight. A paraffin lamp hung on a centre pole inside the tent. Under the light were bicycles, mealie-meal bags, cooking oil containers, cartons of sugar, radios, suitcases, mattresses, shoes, and televisions all thrown together.

An officer, a few metres away from me, shouted instructions that jolted me out of my thoughts. I turned to see a tall man tossing a pen and a clipboard in the air. He seemed outraged. A walkie talkie hung on his chest. A good number of paramilitary officers gathered around him. I walked and stood among the officers. I looked at the face and stared at the name tag on his uniform. Major AB Zulu. I searched for my escort officer. He was not looking in my direction. I broke out of the line and raced towards Major Zulu.

"Major! Major!" I yelled. Major Zulu put his pen in the pocket and stared at me. I stood in front of him, awkwardly.

"Lumba?" he said.

"It's me. Yes. It's me." I said, looking at my box. Officers stared at me suspiciously.

"What brings you here, Lumba?" he asked.

"The clean-up operation, sir."

"What's in the box?"

"A radio. I cannot find the receipt for it." I answered quickly.

"Follow me." I followed the Major, and as we walked, I heard footsteps behind me. Squish-squash. The muddy steps were catching up with us. I did not want to look back.

"Mukuba Mining Corporation is running the emerald mine now?" I enquired.

"Why do you ask?" answered the Major.

"I saw excavators, diggers and loaders on the Shombe Malakata Road. Do they belong to Mukuba Mining Corporation? And are they mining without a licence?"

"They have an exploration licence," said the Major.

"Exploration licence does not allow them to mine," I replied.

"How did you know that?"

"A market vendor said so."

The Major turned to face me. "Who is this market vendor you listen to?"

I did not want to name Micky. So, I was left trying to explain why I should listen to the market vendor. "He's concerned about *Senta*," I put my hand in the pocket and handed him a piece of paper.

"And what is this, Lumba?"

"A Petition."

Major AB Zulu looked at the piece of paper and stared

at me. There was no time to explain to the Major as yells broke out from a distance. An IFA truck had just arrived with a lot of people.

"Did you think for a moment that I would not find you?" said my escort officer when he caught up with us. He looked furious. I turned my gaze away from him and held the petition for the Major to read. He ignored it and gestured for me to move quickly towards the IFA truck that was opposite the burnt Chimanga Changa lorry. Military men ran in the same direction to welcome the new arrivals. They were the unlucky township people from the police cells.

"Process them carefully and move them to Kamfinsa prison. They will be appearing in court tomorrow," said the Major. An officer nodded. The alleged offenders disembarked from the trucks escort officers pulling them by their handcuffed hands.

"What is the matter here? Why is no one acting?" the Major yelled, pointing at a soldier kicking a man. When no one was moving, the Major glared at my escort officer. At first glance, I thought I was dreaming.

"I know him!" I shouted impulsively.

"I did not loot anything..." Hector wailed.

Then I saw my escort officer restraining PC Mambwe and handcuffing him. I hurried towards Hector. His hands cuffed. Staggering, he fell in my arms.

PC Mambwe grumbled, "You must talk to Honourable."

"You are finished private. I am not answerable to anybody in my camp," yelled Major Zulu. At the same time, PC Mambwe was being led away towards one of the tents.

Taking off his coat, the Major laid it on a damp ground.

He removed Hector carefully from my arms and lowered him flat on the garment. Kneeling beside Hector, the Major grabbed more coats from the soldiers standing by and covered him.

"I need an ambulance. A man is bleeding and struggling to breathe. He has a wound on his head. Blood on the face. A swollen face. A broken nose and a cut on the lips. We are at Chamboli Market opposite the burnt Chimanga Changa mealie-meal truck," Major relayed the message on a walkie talkie hanging on his army shirt.

Hector opened his eyes and stared at me. I froze.

"Get me the first-aid box," shouted the Major as soon as he got off the phone. He was commanding and not requesting. And at once, a soldier ran off, and soon returned with a white box. Opening it, the Major took out white bandages. And after cleaning the wound, he wrapped the bandages around Hector's bleeding head. His eyes were watery, lingering on me for a while, and then he looked at Major Zulu. It seemed as though there was no more pain in him.

A distant siren deepened the sombre mood at the market. With a bleeding man lying half-conscious, I felt the ambulance took ages to arrive. Eventually, flashing blue lights and wailing siren surrounded us. The mine ambulance drew up right behind the burnt truck. Then behind the ambulance came a stretcher. I saw the medical team running around the Chimanga Changa truck to where the injured man was.

"I am Doctor Beenzu," she said.

"Major Zulu. I called for the ambulance," he said, holding the side of the stretcher. Doctor Beenzu recognised me and greeted me with her eyes. She turned her head and looked at Hector, who seemed peaceful, and only there was blood on his shirt. Major Zulu had wiped his face and bandaged him. I looked at the Doctor. But I could not tell what she was thinking. She went around Hector, checking his neck.

Then with the help of other medics and Major Zulu, she moved him from the coat to a stretcher. They wrapped blankets around him, as I watched helplessly.

The medics lifted the stretcher, and I followed them. When the Doctor turned around, I looked at her in anticipation, expecting her to speak to me but she didn't. "Anyone to accompany Hector?" asked Doctor Beenzu looking over her shoulder. I looked back and saw my carton box containing my radio waiting for me and decided Hector needed Major Zulu more than me.

I watched the ambulance drive away until the taillights disappeared on the Lwanshimba Road in the direction of the J Section. My panic erupted as the ambulance vanished from my sight. The images of Hector's broken nose and gasping mouth could not leave my mind. I imagined Doctor Beenzu wheeling Hector in her radiology department. She would put him through her scary X-ray machine and test his blood for toxic gases. Being a miner, I worried Hector's blood might show high levels of toxins brought about by *Senta*. His footage would be framed in the nurses' station and added to the collection dated the first of December 1986. The only question was whether she would put a cross or a circle over his lungs. I knelt on the Majors' military coat weeping.

Chapter 31

For two hours, I wandered in the camp with Major Zulu's coat hanging on top of the cardboard box. From the wet slippery path where I was, I heard an argument, "I am not a Malawian. I have shown you my national registration card. What more do you want?" I walked round to the front of the tent and peeped. I saw Mr Phiri waving a national registration card to a young soldier. His youthful looks did not deceive me. A soldier capable of holding captive Mr Phiri was not an ordinary military man.

"Anyone listening to you can tell that you are a foreigner!" said the young officer sternly.

"How can you say that?" shouted Mr Phiri.

"We have been watching you, foreigners. You incited the young men to loot the Chimanga Changa lorry and the shops," the soldier charged. I could not believe he could be so cruel. At once, I began to blame the mining corporation for the troubles of Mr Phiri.

"We are all Zambians here. We have green national registration cards, and we have been here before independence. Before you were born," moaned Mr Phiri. It was apparent to me the officer was indeed born after 1964.

"The Anglo-American Corporation opened the mines here. They forced our ancestors in Nyasaland to leave their wives and their children, to come and work in the mines. They dug copper for the colonial masters for just two shillings a day." Mr Phiri turned and looked in the direction of the mineshaft. My eyes followed what he was looking at: Two big wheels were now motionless on top of the mineshaft.

"The copper ore was hard to break. The picks were blunt. The drilling machines broke down. The spark sticks burnt out. Nonetheless, they dug and drilled, and they fired the sticks until the stones crushed. Our ancestors established the compound," Mr Phiri's eyes shifted to the mineshaft once more.

I stared at the soldier and frowned. When he met my gaze, I quickly pretended I was yawning. I kept my mouth open long enough for him to believe me. What I wanted was to say something. I could not ignore the pain of his mockery and how he treated the men in the tent. What could I say? "Do you know who these men are?" But that has been established. They were miners and children of miners. Did the little soldier know the nobility of a miner who earned the foreign currency for this country? I put my hand over the mouth, took a deep breath to lower my rising emotions.

"Can you hear the ventilation fans from the M Section? Can you hear them? No, they are silent. Do you know why?" said Mr Phiri. I moved closer to hear him well. He continued, "See those chimneys at the Smelter next to the big wheels. There is no smoke, steam, or sulphur dioxide coming out. The gases had been blowing from the pipes since the Anglo-Americans opened the mines for the

British South African Company. Now the mouths of the pipes are dark. They are red like the earth. It is not because of the sun. It is the gases and the heat from the grinders, the stoves and furnace that lie below them. Everything is quiet now because of selfishness."

I could see that the soldier was looking at me, thoughtfully. Then I wondered whether he was now sympathising with the miners and the township people.

"I have seen vibrant miners," Mr Phiri turned round to look at the men sat in the tent. "Today they retire and return to the villages and tomorrow they are coughing. Many are dying in the villages."

There was a long silence, and then the young military soldier glared at me fiercely again. I recognised fury in his expression. Interrupting the hanging silence, the soldier yelled at me. "What are you looking for?" I resisted the urge to run away.

"I need to register my radio!" I replied nervously removing the ITT Supersonic radio and laid it on the table.

"There is no registration going on. Leave the radio."

Mr Phiri and the detainees looked at me hopelessly.

"*Iwe mufana* stop talking in Kiswahili," the soldier charged at the man whispering to Mr Phiri, "What do you have to say for yourself?"

"I took leave to visit my family in Tukuyu and Mbeya," he said in a small cracking voice.

"I have never heard of those villages in Zambia," said the young soldier.

"In Tanzania Bwana. I arrived last night on the Tazara train. I slept in Kapiri Mposhi. I did not participate in the looting," he pleaded.

"You looted the Chimanga Changa and ran away. Huh?"

"No Bwana. I have been away for six months. I came back to my job, and now the mines are on care and maintenance." The man was shaking.

"Here you are!" Major Zulu emerged. "My men have locked up PC Mambwe." He said, facing me as puzzled faces looked back at him.

"Major, I need your help. This man, Mr Phiri, has a green national registration card. It is the same with the rest of the men here. The officer claims they are foreigners and that they incited the market vendors that pushed a wheelbarrow into the Chimanga Changa truck," I said.

I watched the Major stretching out his hand to get the national registration card from Mr Phiri. His eyes were focussed. What he said after made me think he had recognised the village on the identity card. My heart warmed to hear him switch from Bemba to a language that sounded like Nyanja to my ear. Mr Phiri responded in the same dialect. The Major hugged Mr Phiri claiming they were brothers, but Mr Phiri resented the idea. "I am your uncle," said Mr Phiri, "Just look at my age." The two men laughed and embraced the more.

I was nodding and curious if what the two men were saying was real. If speaking the same language made one a member of the same family, I saw much more. I spoke Bemba, and I could not speak a word of Nyanja. I did not like Nyanja that much. Whether that was because the paramilitary men spoke it, or Mr Phiri teased the Bemba speakers I could not tell. Then I thought about Chisenga. Every time I visited him, his grandmother insisted that he should speak in Lala everywhere. However, Chisenga refused, preferring Bemba at home and Lala away from home. It confused me. At the same time, I envied his freedom. The truth is that I loved to hear township people speaking different languages in the compound; Nyanja, Swahili, Bemba, Tonga, Lozi, Ushi, Shona, Mambwe, Kaonde, Lamba and many more.

So then, as I saw things, the NRC did not bother me. All I knew was that we were all township people, even if some loved to go to Tanzania or to Malawi to visit. I counted them as part of the compound. "We all listened to the Masasu band. We attended the J Clinic. We supported the Nkana Football team. We watched games at the Mogadishu Stadium. That is all that mattered to me. Not the language they spoke. Not where the ancestors came from," I thought, and I looked at the miners with gratitude.

Just when I was beginning to enjoy my thoughts, I was interrupted. "Where is the petition?" said the Major after he had calmed down from his prolonged laughter with his newly found relative. I put my hands in the pocket and drew out the piece of paper.

Chapter 32

The morning brought good news. A police car drove on the Kalukungu Road. "The curfew is over. The curfew is over!"

The scenery was that of excitement. Puddles of rainwater lay on the gravel streets. The little children played in the mud. Further along, a group of young boys and girls formed a ring. They clapped their hands, singing and dancing. The warmth of compound life was back. People were moving up and down, and crowds formed and games started.

Everybody down the street was excited. Boys and girls raided garbage bins from the back yards. They beat the containers as they do on the eve of Christmas and the New Year. One or two suckled their babies while they gossiped.

People eavesdropped. Tongues were let loose.

"Major Zulu has arrested PC Mambwe."

"PC Mambwe has met his match."

"The Chief Mine Captain is arrogant."

"Buteko is corrupt."

"The mining company is uncaring!"

Some nodded their heads and said, "This is good for the township."

But words failed me when I looked at the shops. The verandas were empty of people. Passages that lined tailors and shoe repairers were bare concretes. I did not see mini-soccer or flippers. The stores that once flourished with goods were empty shelves, if not burned.

I became aware, once more, of a pain that gripped my heart and the hurt that brought a lump to my throat. I rubbed my eyes and shook my head to steady the throbbing of my brain. I wanted something that would take the pain away. To feel as I did before PC Mambwe arrived in the compound.

Yet, the pain persisted. I feared the township people would never again gather at the Mogadishu Stadium cheering the under-fourteen clubs. I hated the feeling of not waking up to the singing birds or flying grasshoppers. Shop corridors that would never again welcome tailors and shoe cobblers. And fear that I would never again dance with Mwila. It hurt, and I looked away from the ruins.

I met Chisenga among the residents, and we followed a crowd to Chamboli Market.

"This is where I met the Major and where Hector fell into my arms," I said coolly. Chisenga nodded. I felt a gentleness in the air at Chamboli Market. Perhaps it had been there all the time, but I only noticed it now. I looked up at the sky. The sun was emerging behind the cloud.

A little distant from us, there was a small gathering that caught our attention. Chisenga and I joined a crowd watching *isolo*. They marshalled the board to the centre, two men on either side. Women and men sat around, looking at the two men moving small stones from one dip to another. Chisenga and I lowered ourselves on stools. Women watching the game were brewing some tea and roasting some groundnuts on braziers. A bowl of roasted peanuts made rounds, and everyone had a handful. We watched the game in silence, with occasional noise from the chewing.

I met the eyes of one of the men on the side of the board. His hands froze in mid-air after he had scooped the stones. It was his turn to make a move, but he hesitated to spread the pebbles around the board. I resisted the urge to shout.

"This is the man PC Mambwe has been looking for," I whispered to Chisenga.

Chisenga whispered back, "what do you mean?"

A bowl of groundnuts came round again. All the eyes turned on me to do the needful. I quickly got some and passed the bowl to Chisenga who passed it over. Slowly, the man lowered his gaze before he spread the stones that made a massive noise, landing on the board.

"That's the market vendor Mwila failed to coax to leave the compound! Didn't you see him at the library?" I said.
"Of course not!" Chisenga had a searching look. A woman on the reed mat leaned forward and spoke to her colleague in a whisper. Fearing the women had heard us, Chisenga and I walked away from *isolo*.

"That is Katongo," said Chisenga.

"No, Mwila called him Micky. She knows him well."

"He's Mwila's brother! I know Katongo. He is also called Micky," said Chisenga.

I stared at Chisenga in stunned disbelief.

"Are you sure Mwila has a brother?"

"I know her family very well."

"I think the best thing is to try to greet him," I said.

"No. Katongo has not been himself for a long time. Ever since everyone started calling him Micky the Champion, he has kept to himself."

I stared at Chisenga as if he held the keys to the holy grail.

"What is it, Lumba?"

"I do not know who Mwila is," I said, shaking my head in disbelief.

"Mwila is a devoted Catholic. Never missed mass. We were neighbours in the M Section. She took me along to the Seekers, an open bible group. Katongo led it. I have forgotten what happened, but I remember the eagerness with which he began to talk about minerals and the injustices. Each time he told us the stories, I became fearful. Eventually, Father Katyetye replaced him with Peter. Mwila started to miss the mass, and I began to worry about her. Mwila knows I am not a fan of her brother!"

I did not realise he had paused. It was dreamlike, and I did not know how little I knew the people in the compound. It bothered me Katongo looted the mealie-meal truck. It must be him with his champion friends. Now, I wanted to know what Chisenga had forgotten. We endured the silence, broken only by the stones hitting *isolo* board.

"I hope you can remember what happened to him, Chisenga."

"I do not know what to think, Lumba!" Chisenga was shaking his head. His confusion and pain were apparent to me. It was the frustration I saw in Mr Phiri. It also showed in Mwila. I began to imagine it was the same anger that consumed Hector, Mr Patel and the residents that called themselves champions. I could have continued to ask

Chisenga question after question, to make him remember what made Katongo change his name to Micky but I paused. I did not just stand watching the women sipping tea around *isolo*; I was trying to numb the pain.

I waited a while longer before I said, "Surely then, with so much trouble he has wrought on us, he must have a good reason for the troubles?"

"What good is there in pain?"

"Mwila said people do not just loot without reason."

Chisenga quickly answered, "Well, Lumba, I do not doubt that he has a reason. Even when he was leading the Seekers, many of us did not doubt him. Although what he said brought fear, he told the truth. I remember him talking to Mwila and me about children that fell into a pit in the unsecured mine reserve area. It is a scary story whose details I would not want to return to. I worried Mwila would lose interest in the group and obsess herself with the mines injustices."

And with this response, we stared at the lorry in silence. The steam from the cups of tea rose, the smell of groundnuts reached my nose, the sound of the game etched on my mind, I was standing in a market with broken market stalls.

"Did he confess to pushing the wheelbarrow into the lorry?" Chisenga asked. His voice was tense.

"He denied it. I never heard him say anything about pushing the wheelbarrow into the Chimanga Changa lorry."

"But why does Mwila want him gone out of the compound?"

"I do not know Chisenga."

There was a brief silence as we watched Katongo from a distance.

"I finally admitted to Mwila what I had known all along," I said abruptly.

Chisenga replied without much interest, "And what's that, Lumba?"

"I love her," I said, and that got his interest, and he leaned forward.

"What did she say?"

"She accepted my proposal," I replied at once.

"And does this change anything?" asked Chisenga.

"What?" I said.

"Katongo?" asked Chisenga, pointing towards him.

"I don't know him to change anything. Mwila is unpredictable. That I know, she can be casual with the truth, and I know that too. I know that does not answer why she calls her brother a market vendor?" I said weakly.

"Because he is indeed a market vendor," said Chisenga emphatically.

Chapter 33

It would have been hard to believe two weeks ago Chamboli Township had been alive with crowd excitement. But now, it stood empty. It had been twenty-four hours since the police lifted the curfew, but the effects of the past two weeks were not lifting away. The mineshaft alarm did not ring, the ventilation fans were not blowing, and the shops were not open. Everything was still except a sea of debris blew on the Lwanshimba road.

I heard a distant wail of the ambulance siren towards the J Clinic. When the passing ambulance headlights reflected in the rainwater that lay over the surface, I noticed places where there were streetlamps years ago in the days of plenty. I looked along the road, and I saw road markings of white and yellow. Now, they seemed to have greyed with time, and soon they would develop cracks. I worried that there would be potholes and finally the road will be washed away. Then I wondered if It would take another riot to save it.

Although we had a lot to talk about, Chisenga and I walked in silence, each lost in thought until we found Mwila sitting on a bridge, waiting for us. Immediately, the mine police opened the gate. We could hear a bell ringing.

I gave Mwila a sad little smile. "I was called urgently to the clinic because my father had difficult to breathe," said Mwila.

"I am sorry to hear that his condition has worsened," I said gloomily. Mwila took a steadying breath and gave us a sad look. "I also discovered for the first time that father spent two nights in the radiology examination room," she said. Sadness clouded her eyes.

All the ambulances in the parking slots were flashing. The blue lights took me back into the radiology department. I imagined Doctor Beenzu pricking the scaring machine into her father's nerves looking for the signs of poisoning. A cold chill washed over me — thin hairs stood at the back of my neck. Everyone in the compound had experienced the *Senta*. Yet we did not seem too concerned what it did to the residents, rivers, and trees. I looked at Chisenga and wondered if sulphur dioxide was spreading in his body. I closed my eyes briefly, frightened that the compound was addicted to *Senta*. And I feared what would happen if the Mukuba Mining sold the J Clinic.

In the process, I missed a step on the way to the reception. Mwila's hand on mine was spontaneous, as she steadied me. We walked side by side, Mwila and I. She opened the door carefully as if she was avoiding attracting attention to herself. The outpatient department was quiet, and the reception was unstaffed. Once we passed empty chairs in the corridor that led to Mukula Ward, I wondered when Chisenga would be coming to see Doctor Beenzu for the results. I glanced intensely towards the Radiology department, thinking when my turn would be.

Suddenly, a door flung open, and Major Zulu emerged

from the nurses' station. "I saw you from the reception," he said. We stood with eyes wide open. The Major looked at Mwila and Chisenga, and then he looked at me. "Let us go in here!" A worried-looking Major Zulu motioned us to a door.

Following him in a single file, we got into the nurses' station. Doctor Beenzu's desk was empty, Major Zulu offered us seats, and he shut the door behind us. The disinfectant smell of the clinic was very distinct. On the doors and around it were images. "More pictures of broken skulls, arms, ribs and legs had been added to the walls," I said quietly to Chisenga. He nodded, looking at the wall opposite the bench.

"Thank you for coming." The Major's sombre gaze ran over our faces. I lowered my gaze and looked at Mwila and Chisenga from the corner of my eyes. Finding my hand, Mwila tightened her grip on it. I could feel her pulse.

"Can I get you some water?" asked the Major. We nodded, and he handed us a cup each. Water was not enough to cool me down. My heart was beating faster and harder; adrenaline levels rose. I felt the urge to escape, run or hide. I could sense that some terrible news was coming, and I began to get prepared. Part of me almost opened my mouth to Major Zulu to apologise for what had happened to Hector, but I decided not to bother. Although I was almost sure the Zambia Army Officer would listen without threatening me with prison, but that would only be wasting time. It would only mean saying half-truths. I needed to know everything about Micky, who has turned out to be Katongo and why Mwila wanted him to run away. Why was Katongo arousing his champions against Mukuba Mining inside a closed prayer room? Where was he hiding? I needed to know the answers to all these questions and more. Why is he now out of hiding? Was his denial of looting genuine? I wanted to learn more. Not just his threats from the parish and what Chisenga said about him. There must be more to discover about the man that riled the champions in the church library. Whether he pushed the wheelbarrow into the Chimanga Changa truck or not, was not for me to determine now.

I looked at my cup of water again. This time, I wondered if water would wash away my grief and guilt. It seemed to me that the news would not be about Mwila's father. How would the Major know about it? It must be about Hector. If it was about Hector, then it was about Mwila. I longed to go back to when it had all begun. I wished I had persuaded her not to let Katongo go free from the Church library. Admittedly, the guilty must be punished. Why should they be allowed to escape through the holes in the fences? I should not have permitted Mwila to turn my heart against the mining company. I counted my misdeeds, and they were many, and I could not undo any one of them.

I wished there was a way to stop time when evil begins to unfold. We should be able to press a button, set the siren or anything. And better still, we should be able to reverse the time, to replace the bad with the good. If it were possible, I could have taken a different path, although I knew that I had no power to do so. Even now, I did not know how to save the mine township. "We must save the mine township. I will make you understand," Mwila's voice echoed in my mind, and I waited for the bad news.

Major Zulu moved towards the desk and hovered there.

Mwila began to drum her fingers against her trousers. Chisenga was looking at the images of the fractures. I found myself looking at the circles and crosses on the lungs, causing my heart to race even more. I could not help but think of the pregnant woman, worrying if the baby would be born with healthy lungs. Would Doctor Beenzu take pictures of the little lungs? What marks will she put on them? Circles or crosses? I did not want to overthink it. Now, the whole room was a story for me, chaos in the mine township.

I took a deep breath when the army officer turned to me.

"Hector has been moved into the Intensive Care Unit this morning. He is critically ill," he said. The pause that followed was filled in by sighs and sobs.

Chisenga's hand went to cover his gaping mouth. He shuffled his feet and sniffled. Mwila pushed herself further back as if she did not want to be seen. I resisted tears, moved by memories of Hector's injuries.

"Hector suffered internal bleeding. He will never be the same again. Maybe by God's grace, Hector might come through with every limb functioning well and normally," the Major spoke in a quiet, controlled voice. He paused for a moment to catch his breath. My heart began to hurt. I did not know where to turn my anger. Mwila's sniffles turned into sobs. The Major leaned backwards and got a box of tissues. My thoughts were with Hector, lying in Mukula Ward not too far away from us. I bowed my head. In silence, I prayed and prayed for his recovery.

Major Zulu shifted his boots. "I will be retiring from the Army," continued the Major. "My service comes to an end before the turn of December." He put his hands in his pocket and retrieved a piece of paper. "I presented your petition to the Chief Mine Captain and the Honourable MP."

The Major looked overwhelmed. He stretched his hand, and Mwila grabbed it and steadied herself, and we huddled around him. Bidding farewell to the Major with more tears from Mwila, we stepped out of the nurses' station into the corridor.

The signs directly opposite the door showed Mukula Ward. Major Zulu took the direction towards the exit, and we entered the ward.

Chapter 34

Mwila's father was sleeping throughout our visit. We sat around his bed in silence, watching the beeping machine hooked to his hand. A medical card hung on the side of his bed, revealing his condition —Acute Respiratory Constriction.

The message on the medical card made my head spin. The truth is that I feared any disease to do with breathing. The moment I began to suspect sulphur dioxide related ailment, the medical lights in Doctor Beenzu's examination room started to flash in my mind. I wondered if Mwila's father would regain his strength, and I did not want to find out. At least this way, I would be protecting myself from worrying about him, Mwila, Chisenga, Mr Phiri, Hector and myself. We were all connected to the common fate of the dreadful *Senta*.

Chisenga's gaze met mine, and Mwila noticed of our furtive glances. Pulling a leaflet from a drawer next to her father's bed, Mwila handed Chisenga and me one each. We read in silence with the background noise of the beeping machine.

Respiratory conditions prevalent in the mine compound

are associated with high-level exposure to sulphur dioxide. The gas can be life-threatening.

"Sulphur dioxide?" I whispered to Chisenga to avoid disturbing Mwila's father. Chisenga did not appear shaken because he had spent a night here. It was no longer a strange place for him. Since he came out of isolation, we agreed to talk less about it. That's how we decided to cope until Wusakile Mine Hospital would confirm his results. After which, I would test for all ailments connected to sulphur dioxide pollution.

My attention moved to the respiratory machine that kept beeping. It was not flashing like the one in the examination room. It was a steady noise; "beep...beep...beep." I looked up the clock on the wall. I counted a hundred beeps per minute give or take. Then I turned to the leaflet for more information. "The primary environmental health issue in the Copperbelt mining sector is exposure to sulphur dioxide and particulate emissions. The combination of particulate air pollution and the concentration of SO2 is particularly toxic. Smelters emit gases locally referred to as *Senta* which carry sulphur dioxide. There is no air quality control for Chamboli and Wusakile mine townships due to the lack of environmental oversight by the Environmental Agency. In recent years, there has been an increase in cases of deaths from lung infections among retired miners that had moved back to the villages."

"This is the very reason miners do not want to retire to the villages," I told Chisenga in a low tone. He did not react.

"That is the reason Mr Phiri came back to town," Mwila said her gaze to the floor. Silence hung in the air. Until then, I did not realise that Mwila could hear my whispers.

And then Chisenga broke his news. "I am coming back tomorrow for my results from Doctor Beenzu." His voice was calm, almost inaudible.

"And I will also test for the level of metal contamination," I found courage. However, I was dreading the examination process.

A bell began to ring, the sound getting louder and louder. Mwila pulled down the blinds to block the sunlight.

"The Lord keep you," she said. Standing by the side of her father's bed, Mwila hummed a hymn. She was stroking the hand of her father gently. He did not respond.

I got up out of the chair. Everything except the bells and machines in the wing was quiet. Mwila picked up the Gideon bible. She flipped some pages and put it back without reading any text of scripture. Slowly, she rose from the bed. I looked at her. She was looking sad. Saying her quiet goodbye, we headed for the door.

The bell lingered at the ward. Before there was time for us to walk out, the door opened.

"So, you are the one looking after your father now?" asked the bell ringer. He did not step inside the wing; one hand was holding the door, and the other was shaking the bell.

"Yes," Mwila said.

"Where's Katongo?" he asked. Chisenga and I exchanged glances. I thought the ringer was staring at me, possibly wondering if I was here to take the place of Katongo. I could not do that. What if Katongo came back in the night? How would I respond? There was no word from Mwila, and we endured an awkward silence.

After a little hesitation, the ringer stepped back into the

corridor. He resumed his journey, ringing the bell down the hall. We walked in silence behind the bell.

Conscious of a flinging door at the nurses' station, we strolled carefully near it. I saw Doctor Beenzu framing some pictures on the walls. Her gaze met mine, and she beckoned us in. Entering the room, we took seats.

"I asked Katongo to come today." Doctor Beenzu said, drawing an instant response from Mwila, "He is not coming. I do not think he will be coming anytime soon."

I never expected to hear the name Katongo from everyone I met. I was not sure how I felt now. Maybe it was regret, but I could not tell. Chisenga was right. His name is not Micky. Even if Mwila wanted to deny it, the truth is that the man she called Micky was Katongo. I felt duped.

"Your father is responding well to treatment. His upper respiratory tract could not clear sulphur dioxide, which caused him irritation in the nose and throat and caused inflammation of the lower airways. Now that he's doing better and I have amended his lungs mark from a circle to a cross," remarked Doctor Beenzu. Clasping her hands, Mwila nodded gently.

On the table in front of Doctor Beenzu was a folder. Mwila leaned forward to see the text, and Doctor Beenzu pushed the envelope towards her. I thought there was much more coming.

Panic clutched my heart as I gazed at the Doctor. I could not read her mind. Her face scrunched into a questioning expression. I was also watching Mwila without turning my head as my throat was tightening.

"What is inside?" Mwila murmured.

My fears replaced numbness as I began to conjure up

possibilities in my mind. "Mwila's father was in the clinic on the first of December 1986 when we braved the storms. Where was Katongo? Did he go out of the clinic and set the Chimanga Changa lorry on fire? Or was he at the bedside when the looting broke out, and the bell ringer and Doctor Beenzu can alibi him? Does this document convict or acquit Katongo? Am I suppose to say anything about his little rally at the parish? I don't have to say anything. What's certain is Mwila's father suffers from a condition caused by *Senta*. And this report is evidence. The question is—does it contain images of damaged airways hidden from the walls of the nurses' station?"

My mind flickered back to the envelope when Doctor Beenzu pointed to it. "We need to identify miners suffering from lung diseases. Long-serving miners are most likely affected," said Doctor Beenzu. I fixed my gaze to the computer paper, and I got sight of the mine numbers. "The difficulty we have is to locate the retired miners who have returned to the villages," said Doctor Beenzu.

I took in a deep breath before I said, "We need to find Major Zulu before he retires. He can help us." Doctor Beenzu's searching gaze ran over my face. I waited for a response. There was silence. When no one said anything, I spoke slowly, "Major Zulu supervises a roadblock on the Shombe Malakata Road. He knows families of miners that farm along the route. It is a custom that a retiring miner is gifted a piece of land where he grows local produce for his family," I paused. Everyone's eyes were on me. Somehow my mind wondered whether the mabala was to supplement on the lower wages the mining company did not want to raise or the residents just loved to farm. It did not matter to me that I knew the facts well.

"Major Zulu can lead us to the current holders of the mabala, and if we are lucky, we will get the villages of most of the retired miners," I concluded.

"What if Mukuba Mining refuses to treat them?" asked Mwila.

"They should come here. We only ask for a mine number to retrieve records," said Doctor Beenzu.

"What if the mine number was before Mukuba Mining started operations?" Mwila asked.

"If they worked in the mines, they are still miners," Doctor Beenzu said.

"Even when the Anglo-Americans and Cecil Rhodes ran the mines?"

"It does not matter for me. I do keep records," Doctor Beenzu looked at the walls.

"Can they get compensation from current and former mining companies?" I asked.

"I can ask Major Zulu. He's helpful. It should be possible," she said. There was a brief silence. Then Doctor Beezu continued, "Major Zulu was in this morning." Her voice had a reflective tone. "Hector needs an operation," she said what we already knew. "The Major has been helpful to locate Hector's wife and son."

I stared at Doctor Beenzu and did not speak a word glancing at images of the broken bones and damaged lungs framed on the walls.

Chapter 35

*W*hen Mwila led the way through the corridor, her fingers were twitching a bit. She did not look at me, but I took a glance at her. She looked overburdened. She was not her usual confident self. We passed a passage lined up with women on chairs holding medical cards, and next to them were their children. They were waiting for their turn to Doctor Beenzu's radiology department. I wondered how many had respiratory issues. Mwila, Chisenga and I exited the clinic and joined Lwanshimba road. Chisenga bade us goodbye and went his own way.

Now that we were the two of us, I did not know what to say to Mwila. All the reasons not to do anything flooded my mind. I felt I would burst if I did not say anything.

"I met the market vendor," I said. Mwila did not react. It seemed to me that she was pretending not to have heard me, a gimmick she often used to get her way. So, I repeated. "Micky is Katongo, isn't he?" She did not say anything, which made me unsure of myself, and the scenarios I had crafted vanished.

"Can we find a seat somewhere?" she asked.

I began to breathe slowly but inwardly I was wasting

away. I was bumping on the bicycle in the dangerous excavations. A car hit into the bike. If Zempya and PC Mambwe were not beating me, the rain undoubtedly soaked me. Now, I felt betrayed.

We kept on a footpath. The fresh air calmed me, and as we went by in silence, I saw the expecting catholic woman strolling in her green chitenge material. Her fingers were moving fast. I looked up close and noticed a cardigan, bejewelled with copper buttons, and intertwining yellow and white wool extending from her knitting needles. Then I felt sorry for her fingers, neck, shoulders and back. I wondered if knitting was more daunting than mining. There was no more mining. Not at present anyway.

"She has children!" I said after which Mwila looked at me with a blank expression on her face. "Look, she has children. If she is carrying the seventh child, they will not deliver her at J Clinic," I said. Mwila nodded.

The boy that held on to the expectant mother's chitenge material seemed of primary school age. "Remember what your father said," The knitting woman began to say. "This is important. It is not just for your essay at school." She went on to tell stories about how villagers came to work on the mine.

I looked at the boy. He seemed like he was not listening. It seemed to me he was too young to understand what was going on, but the woman continued talking. Mwila and I looked at each other as she spoke loud enough for us to hear.

"Although the villagers had become miners, they held on to some of their village life. They grew maize. Each rain season was an opportunity for them to cultivate the crops in the fields they borrowed from the mines who owned the land. When they retired and did not need the ground, the miners passed the land to the new miners who continued with the tradition. The love for maize would eventually draw milling companies to the region. The milling companies prospered. Chimanga Changa became a big milling company. So, every home in the compound prepared *nshima* every day from the mealie-meal. At the same time, the owners of the mines would say to each other, 'look what the miners eat?' The mine captains mocked the miners. 'The miners don't need a lot of money. They would not know what to do with high wages.' So, the owners of the mines kept the money. And during all this time, the mine operations made the miners and their children sick."

I watched the boy look up to his mother again. He did not ask questions. We walked as if we were in a group of four.

"When the prices of the minerals went up, the mining company wanted more of the minerals. When the prices went down, they needed to sell even more of the minerals. The desire for copper was always in one direction. Up and up and up. As such, they vowed to take on the emerald minefields as well."

I was surprised to see the boy nod his head. I wondered if he knew too that Mukuba Mining Corporation was taking over the emerald mines.

The mother turned back to the boy and said, "Residents have saved the emerald mines and the compound. Our MP, Honourable Mr Buteko has granted their petition against the Mukuba Mining Corporation because of *Senta*." Mwila and I sighed at the same time.

I could not tell what I was feeling. I could sense it was building in me. One moment I thought it was joy, and I wanted to shout and beat my fist in the air. "Finally! They have listened to us." I tried to feel triumphant, but there was nothing to show for it. Then I sensed it was frustration, and my chest tightened. I thought I might explode. I held back the anger when I looked at the boy. The damage was done. I felt sorry for Mwila. I felt sorry for Mr Phiri, and I felt sorry for Mwila's father, I felt sorry for Chisenga. I felt sorry for Hector. I felt sorry for Peter. When I thought of Katongo, I began to fight the tears for the whole compound.

"Hello, do you live…?" She paused and gave me a weak smile. Her eyes looked tired.

"You were looking for Mwila. Is this Mwila?" she asked.

"Yes, she is Mwila," I said at once, and I could see the shock on her face.

"Ah, Mwila! Yes, Mwila! From the M Section?" she asked.

"I lived in the M Section before, and I am in P Section," said Mwila.

"I have not seen you in a long while how you have changed. Do you remember me? I am Ngosa. We were together in the Seekers group. Where is your brother? Katongo? I have not seen both of you at the parish?" she exclaimed. "It's good to see you. This is my son, Hector Junior."

Mwila and I exchanged glances in silence. Words failed me. I stared into the boy's little brown eyes looking a bit lost.

"Do you know Hector? Heard about Hector on the radio?" Ngosa asked. Knowing her name did not help me.

Even before she uttered the next word, I could tell where it was going. I saw her lips move. My mind was blank, and my eyes widened as I stared at the poor little boy and the mother in horror. I wanted to apologise. To say how sorry I was for the contributions I had made to her troubles. Whether Mwila shared my guilt or not, I could not tell, but it was of no use to Ngosa for me to allocate blame.

I held my breath even before she said, "My husband is undergoing surgery at J Clinic." I had to say something! I searched my mind for something consolatory to say. Still, to my surprise, my heart answered for me, "I'm sorry, Ngosa, and I'm sorry, Hector Junior."

"There are prayers for him at the parish this evening," said Ngosa resuming her journey with her boy. I turned back and saw Ngosa and Hector Junior enter the J Clinic.

"How well do you know Ngosa?" I asked Mwila.

"She used to work in the Church library," said Mwila holding my hand. "I don't know what she does at the parish now."

The gate at the Mogadishu Stadium lay ajar. Pushing it open, we climbed the terraces. Mwila led the way, her hand in mine, to the seats we once shared. Settling down, we said nothing to each other and stared at an empty ground. The sun lowered behind Nkote Club, leaving behind red clouds in the horizon, the shadows of the mutuntulwa trees fell in the centre of the field, and the wind blew gently on my face.

"When I was small, my father used to bring me here," Mwila said slowly and softly. I touched her arm, and she gently put her head on my legs and looked up as if she were dreaming.

"That's how I came to love the Little Chiefs Football

239

Club. I watched every match on the shoulders of my father."
A smile touched the corners of her mouth. I smiled too.
Then her smile became tender until remorse came on her
face.

"I was devastated when Doctor Beenzu admitted my
father to the clinic. He needed someone to care for him. I
chose to go to university. Katongo chose to look after him."
Mwila was fighting tears. "Katongo gave up his stand at the
market. So, no, Katongo is not a market vendor anymore.
His friends know him as Micky. I call him Micky when I
want to please him. I feel guilty that I went to university,
and he gave up his livelihood." Mwila lifted her head off
my leg and stared at the centre of the ground.

"Katongo was devastated when he learnt that our
father's sickness was because of the exposure to the *Senta*."

I searched her face for anger, but I saw calmness.

"Katongo worries that our father's case would be like
Mr Phiri's."

"What case?"

"Mr Phiri retired some years ago and moved back to
the village. Later, the doctors diagnosed him with a lung
disease caused by exposure to sulphur dioxide. For the lack
of specialised treatment in the village, he returned to the
Copperbelt. Still, the Mukuba Mining Corporation cannot
admit him to the J Clinic," Mwila paused. My mouth felt
dry, and my knees weak.

"When I arrived home three weeks ago, Katongo
showed me a redundancy letter of our father," she continued.
And I gasped.

"The Chief Mine Captain signed the letter dated a

few weeks ago," she added. I did not know what to say to comfort her.

"Katongo dislikes Mukuba Mining Corporation and the Chief Mine Captain," she said. Her voice was cracking with emotions, tears rolling down her face.

"Can the Honourable help?" I enquired.

"Lumba, he has done nothing. I am not sure how long the petition will hold," she said.

"Major Zulu? Doctor Beenzu?" I asked.

"They are our only hope now," she said. An extended period of silence followed. And when she looked at me again, her eyes were clear. I gathered her in my arms and held her tight.

"You are strong and beautiful," I said.

"You have never said that to me," she said and lowered her eyes.

"But it is true," I insisted.

"The first time I saw you I said in my heart, she is beautiful. She is the most beautiful girl I have ever seen."

I noticed her tired face disappeared, and her eyes lost their sadness. Mwila smiled and stared into space. We sat quietly for a moment.

Then, there were melodies of birds singing, and the rustling of the leaves of the mutuntulwa trees. I closed my eyes, holding Mwila tightly, in the gentle wind from the forest.

It was a moment of supreme tranquillity. I could hear Mwila's heartbeat as the birds ended their singing. "No woman, no cry" resounded in my mind. I had not listened much to Bob Marley ever since I knew Mwila. All the songs I would later know were done by the Serenje Kalindula band or the Masasu band. I opened my eyes and gazed at her. She was looking up in the sky as the leaves sprinkled on the pitch.

"Is Mr Buteko a Zambian?" I asked.

"What do you mean?" she said.

"I thought everyone is a Zambian whichever side of the mineshaft their home is! Hmm. Smile, forgive and forget and be a little bit more Zambian!" I said. Mwila laughed and laughed and laughed.

I studied her face. She was serene, and I felt attracted to her cheeks and kissed her for the first time. She did not protest.

Dark and heavy clouds gathered over the ground casting darkness for a short time causing the stadium lights to flicker randomly. When the lights became steady, the rain started to drizzle. Mwila pushed her umbrella open. I got the umbrella from her and held it in one hand. Wrapping her arm around my shoulders, we walked out of the stadium through the gate opposite the L Section. Mwila turned and closed the gate. It would be the last time the stadium was opened to the township.

Author's Note

*C*haos in the Mine Township is a work of fiction based on real events. There is indeed a beautiful mine township called Chamboli in Kitwe, the biggest town on the Copperbelt in Zambia. Chamboli is located a few kilometres from the mineshaft and smelters, where the giant mining corporations extract copper and release toxic gas *Senta* into the local population.

If you had visited Chamboli and the sister mine township, Wusalike, in the 1980s, during the time the story relates, you would have seen green trees everywhere. When it rained, and it did in fact rain, the sound was musical. More often after a storm, the sun would emerge, flowers would blossom, birds would sing, and *inswa* and *inshonkonono* would soar in the clear sky. Every evening, music played from taverns. At specific times of the day and night, the mine alarm sounded to announce the change of shifts. These are historical facts, and I have not changed them.

However, I have fictionalised some events and places. There was no shop called Fyonse General Dealers nor Asian Shopping Stores, and I felt free to change the name of the mining company. I want to acknowledge the deal to sale an emerald mine was my invention, and it did not happen as told in the story.

But in some places, the book retains real names such as Mogadishu Stadium, J Clinic, Nkote Club, Mwabonwa Tavern, and Chamboli Parish. Still, nothing said about these, and other real places could be considered offensive. I had a lot of options for the name of the looted milling truck and its location, and I chose the most likely possibility, namely Chimanga Changa at Chamboli Market.

All persons named are not real, except for President Kaunda and the sports personalities, whom I have celebrated their contributions to the pride of the city of Kitwe. In no case is the reference to a position intended to an actual holder.

Whether the leading cause of the riots was the decline in the copper prices, or something else is not for this book to reveal. The reasonable impact on the lives of the people who lived in the compound is hard to estimate. Therefore, the extent of damage, the number of casualties, the amount of *Senta*, the number of *Senta* sufferers, the level of pollution to the Kamatemate River and the destruction of the Milemu forest could have been less than the book portrays.